You met District Attorne[...] in
#379 *Partners for Life*. R[...]
Fontaine Woman! where he discovers that his most
bitter enemy is the woman of his dreams.

"You Want Me, Adam."

Diana saw the flicker deep in his eyes and knew she'd
scored a direct hit. "Yes, I can see it, and sense it.
A woman always knows when a man's interested in
her. Unfortunately, I'm the wrong woman. It
disturbs you to think that lightning can strike twice,
doesn't it? You don't want to believe you can want
me the same way your mother wanted my father."

Adam knew he was an inch away from doing
something drastic and should put her away from
him; he knew that he was sealing his own fate by not
listening to his instincts, but she was right—he
wanted her, and having it a spoken thing between
them made desire flare all the more quickly, blocking
out everything but need.

"You're damned sure of yourself," he said, knowing
how it would provoke her and cancel any retreat for
either of them.

"I'm sure of both of us," she whispered, and
pressed her lips to his.

Too late, she realized her folly. He was ready for her.

Dear Reader:

Happy New Year!

It takes two to tango, and we've declared 1989 as the "Year of the Man" at Silhouette Desire. We're honoring that perfect partner, the magnificent male, the one without whom there would *be* no romance. January marks the beginning of a twelve-month extravaganza spotlighting one book each month as a tribute to the Silhouette Desire hero—our *Man of the Month*!

Created by your favorite authors, you'll find these men are utterly irresistible. You'll be swept away by Diana Palmer's Mr. January (whom some might remember from a brief appearance in *Fit for a King*), and Joan Hohl's Mr. February is every woman's idea of the perfect Valentine....

Don't let these men get away!

Yours,

Isabel Swift
Senior Editor & Editorial Coordinator

HELEN R. MYERS
That Fontaine Woman!

Silhouette Desire

Published by Silhouette Books New York

America's Publisher of Contemporary Romance

SILHOUETTE BOOKS
300 East 42nd St., New York, N.Y. 10017

ISBN: 0-373-05471-8

First Silhouette Books printing January 1989

Printed in the U.S.A.

Books by Helen R. Myers

Silhouette Desire

Partners for Life #370
Smooth Operator #454
That Fontaine Woman! #471

Silhouette Romance

Donovan's Mermaid #557

HELEN R. MYERS

lives on a sixty-five acre ranch deep in the piney woods of east Texas with her husband, Robert, and a constantly expanding menagerie. She lists her interests as everything that doesn't have to do with a needle and thread. When she and Robert aren't working on the house they built together, she likes to read, garden and, of course, outfish her husband.

To R.C., M.T., and the girls they fell for,
Beth and Chris,
with love.

One

She had done it again.

Adam Rhodes stormed into his office and slammed the door behind him. After flinging off the navy blue jacket of his three-piece suit, he headed straight for the bar. With clipped, sure moves he poured two fingers of Scotch into a crystal tumbler, skipped the ice he usually preferred, and gulped the drink down in one lethal swallow. The fiery alcohol had the expected and desired effect on his empty stomach: first it burned like hell, then he went numb inside. Now, he thought, if only his mind would be half as obliging.

He began reaching for the bottle again before he caught himself. Grimacing, he set down the empty glass and crossed over to his desk where he dropped into the black leather chair and rubbed his hand up and down his face. God, she was turning into a one-woman crusade intent on sending him to the funny farm. It was the only explanation that made any sense for this latest *coup de main*. Shuffling through the stack of files and phone messages on his desk, he found the interoffice memo he'd been told about clipped to its appropriate file. The latest surprise attack had been the case of Carlos Madera, a parolee who had just been rearrested for the burglary at 1137 San Pedro. She was taking on the case pro bono—what else was new?—and was making counterclaims of harassment, and threatening to file charges of police brutality!

"The hell you are," he muttered, reaching for the phone. "Get me Diane Fontaine. *Now*." This time she'd gone too far. Once and for all, he was going to wipe that smart-aleck smile off her face. Madera was as guilty as if he'd been caught with his hands in the proverbial cookie jar. His butt was going back to Huntsville posthaste.

"I'm sorry, Mr. Rhodes," Muriel Littlejohn said, interrupting his silent fulminations. "Ms. Fontaine is out of the office and isn't expected back until noon."

"It's twenty after."

"I'm aware of that, sir," his secretary replied with a nasal twang he swore she emphasized because she knew it irritated him. "I'm only telling you what her secretary told me. Do you want to leave a message?"

Adam closed his eyes, which only served to magnify Muriel's image in his mind. He could see her sitting beyond the oak door, patting her beehive hairdo in place, though it would take a tornado to disrupt it. He could even visualize the expression of unrivaled suffering that would undoubtably appear on her full-moon face.

"If it isn't going to be an inconvenience," he said sarcastically, "tell her to call me. No. Tell her I want to see her. Today."

Belying her age, Muriel snapped her gum. "Uh-huh."

When Adam replaced the receiver onto the phone's cradle, he did it with a force he hoped would shock her into swallowing the stuff. He and Muriel did not get along. It had nothing to do with the fact that she was as old as the building they inhabited—he even had his suspicions she'd come with the place—and was nearly as large; it was that she treated him as if *he* were the one who should toe the line or else start perusing the classified-ad section of the morning paper. In the three years he'd been district attorney of Corpus Christi, he'd had to fight her on every administrative change made. "This isn't the way Mr. Freemont used to do it. That isn't what Mr. McDonald would have liked," she would say. He should have let her go when he first wanted to, instead of listening to all the advice urging him to keep her and not risk an Employment Commission investigation. Now it had become a test of wills to see who was going to drive out whom first.

"Damned conspiracy," he muttered, slumping deeper into his chair. If he didn't know better, he would have suspected that Fontaine woman of planting his secretary here to purposely help drive him nuts; but Diana had only been back in town for six months. Granted, in that time she'd managed to drive his entire staff crazy with her maverick trial maneuvers, but as far as he knew, she hadn't tried to infiltrate the place with spies— yet.

As his thoughts refocused on Diana, he picked up the Madera file again. His best man was on the case; Phil Gresham was as thorough and persevering as Diana was. Surely he hadn't missed something before Madera was even arraigned? If there was anything he hated more than losing a case—when it was obvious the defendant was guilty—it was losing because of a mistake. From the moment a suspect was given his Miranda reading and acknowledged he understood his rights, to the mountain of documentation it took to get him to trial, there were, admittedly, innumerable ways for errors to occur—any of which could put the suspect back on the streets. But Adam didn't abide with much of it. Sure, the system was flawed; sure, it was drowning in its own paperwork; but it was the only system they had, and he intended that it be followed or else.

As much as he hated to admit it, Diana Fontaine, and all defense attorneys like her, were the checks and balances to his office. They served a fair and necessary function, but she carried it to excess. He was certain that with her, winning a case against the D.A.'s office was a personal thing. After all, she was a Fontaine and he was a Rhodes. An old feud had caused a gulf between their families deeper than the Grand Canyon. Beating him professionally was simply her way of getting in a few more punches on her father's behalf. Over the past six months Adam had watched her turn nearly a dozen cases into wins for her clients. If he honestly believed she took the cases because she'd been convinced of her clients' innocence, it wouldn't be leaving such a bad taste in his mouth. But he doubted there was one sincere bone in that elegant body, and that riled him about as much as his helpless attraction to her angered him.

He could still remember that evening last November when he'd arrived at Judge Halliday's home for the annual Thanksgiving party that had always been the legal social circle's unofficial kickoff for a manic month of celebrating. He'd walked into the dimly lit room and found himself staring at the back of a woman he instantly knew he wanted to meet. She'd been dressed in a gray velvet creation that draped seductively low on the loveliest back he'd ever seen. It made him forget all about not having wanted to go out on that rainy night. As he crossed the room toward her, he'd found himself hoping she looked half as good from the front, wasn't wearing a wedding ring, and had an IQ reasonably close to intelligent. That he'd long been avoiding a serious relationship was testament to her effect on him.

She'd been everything he hoped for, all right, but there had also been a kicker: she was L. C. Fontaine's daughter, come home after several years of practicing in Boston to join Daddy's law firm. Adam could still recall how the shock had been as startling as a sudden ice bath. *She* hadn't seemed too affected, though. She merely gave him that damned smile he would come to know all too well, and coolly said something about being pleased to see him again after all these years. She also told him she was looking forward to working in his jurisdiction. He'd been dodging thrusts and jabs from the press who were enthusiastically following her as she blitzkrieged his assistants in court ever since.

But this time she wasn't going to get away with it. He'd had enough, and he was going to send her a clear message to that effect.

He reached for the phone again. When Muriel came on the line, he demanded, "Has she called yet?"

"Wouldn't I have told you if she had?"

He wondered. "Call again. Then ring Gresham and tell him to get in here."

He hung up and jerked his tie loose. So much for his idea about squeezing in a quick game of racquetball during his lunch hour. Maybe it was just as well; in his mood he would probably send the ball straight through concrete.

There was a short rap on the door and then a harried-looking man, close to Adam's own age, poked his head in. He took one look and sighed. "Fearless Fontaine?"

"Who else?"

"Lord have mercy on this soul of mine," he murmured under his breath, and entered at a less-than-enthusiastic pace.

Diana Fontaine walked into the offices of Fontaine, Danning, Fontaine & Associates and was met by several cheers and one creative interpretation of the theme song from *Rocky* hummed through a paper rolled up like a megaphone. She gave them a formal bow before circling the clerks' and secretaries' desks to head toward her office. It never ceased to amaze her how quickly news traveled in this business.

"Better not let Brother Oscar see you wasting company money," she drawled, as she passed the musician.

Grinning, the young clerk unrolled the sheet of paper. "I beat him at his own game. I've recycled his memo where he complains about too much paper being wastefully shredded."

"We've heard that, Mr. Foster, and we are not amused," came a frosty pronouncement from behind them.

Diana and the startled clerk turned around to face the small, sad-eyed man who did, indeed, look more like a Franciscan monk than an attorney. There wasn't a person in the office who didn't silently groan when they saw Oscar Danning coming toward them. He had the ability to generate as much enthusiasm as an IRS audit with his memorandums about conserving manpower and office supplies; however, after careful study Diana had concluded that the firm somehow replaced the family he didn't have. All that nagging and nit-picking wasn't unlike a mother's telling a child to stop slouching or stop feeding vegetables to the dog under the table; and because of that, she'd been able to find his eccentricities more amusing than irritating.

She hooked her arm through his and drew him away from Foster. "Lighten up," she coaxed. "I made us a half million today on the Wilkinson case. Now you can afford those plastic runners you wanted to get to protect the carpeting."

"Laugh if you will," he replied, in his usual dignified manner. "I've estimated those runners will save us approximately four hundred dollars a year in cleaning costs."

"No! That much?"

"Diana, as a partner in this firm, it would behoove you to show a little more respect and interest in what it costs to operate it. Then, perhaps, you'd find the inclination to take on more clients like Wilkinson instead of those pro bonos you're so fond of."

As they paused before her secretary's desk, Diana gave him a tolerant smile. "Oscar, dear, I keep as close an eye on my portfolio as anyone else does, and I'm still the firm's top earner, despite my gratis work."

He drew himself up to his maximum height, which should have topped hers, but because she was wearing three-inch heels, he still found himself having to tilt back his head to meet her eyes. "There's nothing shameful about using money as a basis for judging one's success."

"Nor is there anything wrong with gauging it by the number of people you can help while still keeping the bills paid. Either way, I would think both of us should be well satisfied."

He sighed, knowing better than to try to rationalize with her when she was pumping adrenaline from a fresh coup. "I suppose I should tell you before anyone else does, that L.C. was in this morning," he murmured, changing the subject.

The smile on her face quickly gave way to a frown. "That old fox. He knows the doctor said he could come in twice a week, but not more. I've a mind to haul his stubborn bones in for a checkup, even though he's not due for another week. Then we'll see how clever he thinks he's being."

"That's probably why he said to be sure to tell you not to call him during the afternoon. He said he was going to be lying down and resting." He and L.C. had been partners for over twenty-five years. As frugal as he was, Oscar knew he would never have achieved the success he had without the gutsy older man. Impulsively, he touched Diana's hand. "He's already given up so much. He's got to be allowed a little pleasure."

"I'm only trying to buy him the time the doctors say he could have if he behaves himself." In a gesture of helpless frustration, she lifted her hand, then dropped it.

"It's not easy when everyone's right, is it?"

She swallowed the lump that rose unexpectedly in her throat and shifted her leather briefcase into her other hand. "No plastic runners in my office, Oscar."

He gave her a brief, rare smile before going on about his business. Diana squared her shoulders and turned to her secretary.

"Hi. Come on in and tell me what else is going on," she said, leading the way into her office.

Andrea Cole grabbed her stenographer's pad and sprang to her feet. "You-Know-Who called. I think he probably heard about the Madera case and wants his pound of flesh, since he thinks you owe him for allowing Seals to get his sentence reduced to a probation."

"A pound is out. I missed lunch," she explained, winking at the gamin-faced, petite woman. She laid her briefcase on the corner of her desk, slipped off her red, bolero-cut suit jacket and hung it neatly on the brass coat stand in the corner. "Besides, the Seals probation was no favor; we saved the taxpayers by doing what a trial would have done, anyway. Though I have to admit I've been expecting him to— Four? He's called four times in the last three hours?" she asked, picking up the pink phone messages.

"I told you he was hot under the collar."

Diana sat down on the edge of her desk and fanned herself with the small squares of paper. A slow, wicked smile pulled at her generous mouth and relit the sparkle in her eyes. "Okay...good. What else?"

The younger woman gaped, clearly unnerved. For a moment she fidgeted with her narrow tie. "Aren't you going to call him?"

"Eventually," Diana murmured, shifting to check her appointment calendar. "Those people from Federated are coming in shortly, aren't they? I told them corporate counsel wasn't my forte, but I'd like to personally introduce them to Roger and sit in on the initial meeting. Oh—right. That retirement party for Judge

Perry is tonight. I'll talk to our illustrious district attorney then, after he's had a chance to cool down a bit with a martini or two.''

"You *know* he only drinks Scotch."

With unconscious sensuality, Diana ran the tip of her tongue along the rim of her upper teeth. "By tonight he'll be ready for martinis." She tossed the messages into the wastebasket at her feet and drew out her red-framed reading glasses from her briefcase, which were considered a signature as much as the long, double string of pearls she almost always wore. "All right, let's get this show on the road. Call Rose and ask her if she'd lay out my black Victor Costa before she leaves for the day, then call Martin and find out if he's still planning to pick me up. You can have this stack of letters back to mail in five minutes, and I'm finished with those files on the credenza. What else have you got for me, Andy?'' she asked, moving from the desk to the navy blue executive chair behind it.

"Nothing that can't wait until morning."

"Come again, remind me that I can't survive without you."

"With pleasure. How about a cup of lemon tea with honey to give you a little energy boost?"

"Yuck. I'll take a diet whatever, though."

"And the granola bar I have in my drawer?"

"I have a chocolate bar in mine."

"You're weird," Andrea muttered, picking up the files. "I don't know how you manage to keep that complexion and figure with the junk you eat."

"To each his own, kiddo. By the way, I like the tailored shirt and tie with that leather miniskirt. Contradictory but chic."

"It's my protest against Mr. Danning's dress code."

"I'm sure he's too busy looking at your legs to notice," Diana drawled, scrawling her signature across the top letter in the stack of outgoing mail.

A few minutes later, after Andrea brought her the soft drink and took away the signed letters, Diana sat back for a moment to catch her breath from the hectic day that was far from over. The need for moments like this was one of the main reasons she'd had her office decorated primarily in blue. Blue calmed, she thought, taking in the indigo-blue walls and powder-blue carpeting. So did the huge unframed painting hanging over the mauve couch. It was a picture of outer space with a mauve, crater-riddled moon occupying the upper fourth of the canvas and millions of stars sprinkling the rest. She'd been instantly drawn to the piece at an arts-and-crafts show, though it was as opposite to her usual tastes as she could get. One look at it and she knew it was exactly what she needed for her office for times when she was trying to make sense of a world she rarely thought sane at all.

Like now. Adam was ready to do battle over the Madera case, and why? Because he couldn't accept her being right about it—or about anything, for that matter. It was crazy. His anger had nothing to do with justice, any more than it did with the other cases he butted heads with her on. This was about old ghosts; old hurts that as far as she was concerned were ancient drivel she had no intention getting involved in. As for Adam himself, however, that was a different story.

There was something else between them, and it was a lot more interesting than skeletons in the closet, Diana thought, smiling secretively. There was chemistry—a volatile, white-hot something that was going to have to be dealt with one day whether they wanted to or not.

Diana knew it was the other half of the reason why he behaved like an ornery bear around her; he didn't like the idea of being attracted to her. She wasn't exactly thrilled with it herself, but at least she'd had a longer chance to adjust. She'd had a crush on him when she was a teenager. Luckily, college, law school and then their careers had pulled them half a continent apart and helped to let her almost forget him. But now she was back, and it was obvious this wasn't kid stuff anymore.

Maybe if they'd dealt with it openly and honestly, as she would have preferred, they would be laughing about it now. But from the moment of their reunion, Adam couldn't seem to get beyond a civil greeting, and things had been going downhill ever since. Admittedly, she was to blame for much of it. She took a wicked pleasure in dangling the metaphoric apple beneath Adam's nose and watching him squirm, or rather, steam. She would do so again tonight. If it was a contest of willpower he wanted, so be it. But they were going to play by her rules.

The buzz of her intercom brought her back out of the depths of space and, blinking, she picked up the phone. "Yes, Andy?"

"The people from Federated are walking through the front door."

"I'm on my way."

She hung up and stood. Reaching for her jacket, she mentally ticked off the names of the officers of the corporation, refreshing them in her mind, as she always did, to memorize the names of new clients. She was halfway to the door when she felt her stomach pull with hunger. Belatedly she remembered the chocolate she hadn't gotten around to eating. Retracing her steps, she quickly downed the rest of the soda in the Styrofoam cup, then tossed it into the trash. Once again, her glance fell on the pink telephone messages. It made her smile all the more naturally as she went out to greet her visitors.

Two

I love spring," Diana mused, hours later, as she sat beside Martin Prescott while he drove them to the country club. "It always reminds me of that line about taking time to smell the flowers. There are so many flowers in the spring."

"And so little time to enjoy them all," he said, finishing for her. "My, we're becoming philosophical in our old age." But the glance he shot her across the confines of the BMW was affectionate. They were the same age, had in fact gone to school together. He knew neither of them really felt old; at times it was hard to even remember they were thirty-three already.

"It must be this retirement party. I remember when Uncle Bernie used to let me drive his golf cart back to the clubhouse on Sundays. He and L.C. had to take me with them because Rose had the morning off to go to church. I had my own set of clubs and they used to make me practice putting into a paper cup while they each took their shots.''

"With that kind of tutelage you should've become a professional.''

"I discovered swimming instead, remember?''

"Ah, yes, and became the legend of the Westbrook swim club without ever having competed in a race. I'll bet you still look good in a wet bikini.''

She smiled at him, taking in his dark hair and clean profile. The wire-frame glasses were new and had been her suggestion when he told her he'd been for an eye exam and had been told his vision was no longer perfect. He'd been leaning toward contact lenses, but she suggested he also get a pair of glasses, because she thought they would give him an attractive, intellectual look. As usual, she'd been right about what was good for him. It had never been necessary to actually say it, but she loved him. She'd often wished they'd been born siblings—being best friends was the next best thing.

"Martin, pull into that Dairy Queen up ahead and let me get a cone.''

"Are you serious? We're a mile from the club.''

"It was one of *those* days. Right now the steering wheel is beginning to look appetizing. Besides, you know there'll be a half hour of mingling before we get near any food.''

"Let me know if you feel faint, and I'll grab your elbow, but I'm not pulling up to the valet parking area with you wolfing down an ice-cream cone. Remember that orange you had to have at the Christmas benefit concert? People still think it's hilarious to use my pockets as their personal Dumpster.''

She watched the fast-food restaurant come and go.

Humor replaced the look of indignation on Martin's face. "Ever try looking at a man the way you look at junk food?"

"Put it in your ear, Prescott. When was *your* last date?"

"Yesterday." His smile was smug.

She whipped around in her seat. "Who?"

"Lisa."

Diana's skepticism turned to delight. "Lisa said yes? Martin, that's great!" Lisa was his secretary of two months. He'd fallen head over heels for her the moment she walked into his office for the job interview and would have hired her if she'd typed with two fingers. Unfortunately, he learned too late that she didn't believe in accepting dates with her employer, and he'd been brooding about what to do ever since. "What happened?" she demanded.

He shot her a speaking glance, which she dismissed with a wave of her hand. "Stop being so literal. I mean *how* did you pull it off? Where did you take her?"

"I thought about you and resorted to devious tactics."

"Wait a minute—"

"Remember that lifeguard the summer before you turned sixteen?"

"Oh." In the last rays of daylight, her gray eyes began to sparkle. "God, I was good, wasn't I?"

Martin cleared his throat. "Anyway, I had to improvise, but the principle was the same. I told Lisa I was having dinner with a client who had to give a deposition but couldn't come to the office during regular hours. She agreed to come along to take it down."

Diana was clearly disappointed. "She didn't fall for that one, did she?"

"Not for long," he admitted, pulling through the gates of the country club. "But after I did some quick explaining and apologizing, she decided she could find some humor in the whole thing and agreed to stay for dinner. I think I'm in love, Di."

"Either that or the prescription in those glasses is off; you almost ran over that parking attendant."

They got out of the car and Martin sheepishly apologized to the young man with the quick reflexes. When he joined Diana on the front steps, she burst into laughter and hugged him.

"You're terrific. Are you going to let me be best man at your wedding? I think I'd lend a certain something to a tuxedo."

"Don't be in such a hurry. I don't want to make any more mistakes with her than I already have, and anyway...you *would* wear one, wouldn't you?" He shook his head, then drawled, "I guess it would be safer to cover as much of you as possible. That's some dress, Counselor."

The black velvet-and-taffeta strapless sheath delineated the subtle curves of her slender body and was accented by an oversize taffeta bow at the back.

"I didn't ruin it in the car, did I?" she asked, turning to let him check it for her.

"You're leaning a little to portside. Hold still a second and I'll—"

"I thought the entertainment came *after* the speeches."

At the sound of that cold, sarcastic voice, Martin groaned softly into Diana's ear. "Don't look now, but I think the iceman cometh."

Diana drew a deep breath and turned to give the man on the lower step a regal smile. "Hello, Adam. Jumping to conclusions, as usual, I see."

Martin winced and quickly extended his hand. "How are you, Adam? I understand you shot a hole in one here last weekend. Off the eleventh, wasn't it? That one's always my weak spot. Er—we're running a bit late. Why don't we go on it?"

Before anyone could say anything else, he grabbed Diana's wrist and pulled her up the rest of the steps and inside. They were soon swallowed up by the crowd that had come to celebrate Judge Perry's retirement; but that didn't stop Martin from shooting a wary glance over his shoulder.

"All right, what is it this time?" he whispered into her ear.

Diana smiled and nodded to a couple who passed them. "Whatever do you mean?"

"I saw the way he looked at you. That man's out for blood—yours—which can mean only one thing. What did you do to tick him off this time? No, on second thought, I don't think I want to know. As it is, I'm already considered guilty by association. I don't want to add collusion to the list."

"Why is it always assumed that whenever he's in a particularly grim mood, it's my fault?"

"Maybe because you, more than anyone else, are able to find his Achilles' heel." He spotted the end of the reception line and led her over to it.

"That's neither kind nor fair," she whispered back in protest. "You know I'm only doing my job the best way I know how. Can I help it if he takes it all as a personal attack?"

"All I'm saying is I hope you know what you're doing."

Someone from Martin's own law firm stopped to speak with him and Diana used the opportunity to glance around the lobby for Adam. Knowing he scorned lines, she didn't bother looking over her shoulder. He was the type who would wait until everyone else had paid their respects and gone inside to the banquet room before approaching the guest of honor himself.

Sure enough, she spotted him across the lobby talking to the chief of police and exchanging one glass of champagne for another from the tray a passing waiter held. She smiled inwardly as she felt the tension in him radiate across the room like heat waves. It had never occurred to her to think it odd that a man who gave the impression of such coldness could also seem capable of a passionate temperament that bordered on white-hot. But she agreed with everyone who said he was one of a kind.

Adam Barclay Rhodes should have been born a monarch, she mused, taking in the striking figure he cut in his dark formal wear. He had that indefinable something that set the aristocracy apart from the rest. Coupled with his sharply sculpted features and almost Nordic coloring, the effect was quite formidable. But Diana left the tendency to being intimidated to others. She knew her own abilities and attributes too well to allow him any psychological upper hand.

They were both products of proud, ambitious families whose ancestors were among the first settlers in Texas. Early on, her people made their fortune in cattle ranching and then oil, before spreading that power base to law. Adam's forefathers championed in commerce and banking before shifting their considerable

influence toward politics. Their fathers had once been
the best of friends, for years living as neighbors in the
most fashionable district in town. Time and turmoil had
changed things considerably. Their numbers were fewer,
their power was less than it was and the friendship had
ended abruptly. But they were still affluent and their
names still marked them as part of the socially promi-
nent. The difference between them was that Adam liked
it that way, and Diana found it a mixed blessing.

Not that he liked socializing, Diana thought, almost
chuckling as two more people joined him and the police chief. By the pained look on his face, she would
wager they'd had the audacity to change the subject
from business to something far more superfluous. Poor
man, this wasn't his day.

"Would you mind wiping off the Cheshire-cat
smile?" Martin pleaded. "We're next."

"I can't wait for Lisa to take my place as your lucky
companion to these soirees," she whispered back.

"You'll miss me and you know it. But maybe you and
Adam can make it a foursome. He hasn't been seen with
anyone steady since that little blonde last year."

"What little blonde?"

"Martin. Diana, my dear. So good of you to come."

Diana was forced to forget her question and turned
to the trim, silver-haired retiring judge. "Uncle Bernie,
you look wonderful," she said, accepting his affectionate peck on her cheek. "Far too young to retire."

"That's why I want him out," said his wife, Emily,
beside him. Small and somewhat plump, she beamed
warmly at Diana and took her hands in her own.
"Twenty years is enough on the bench. I told him it's
time he took me on a cruise before he forgets about romance altogether. How's L.C., dear?" she added more

softly. "We're so sorry to hear he's still under the weather."

Diana kept her smile bright. "He's better, thanks. He told me to be sure and give you his best."

"Tell him he needs to start taking more vitamins, like I do," Judge Perry advised.

In response, Emily rolled her eyes. "He wouldn't remember to take them himself if I didn't lay them beside his juice glass every morning."

"Speaking of drinks," Martin said, "Diana and I are going to hunt one down before the bar dries up." He slipped an arm around her waist and led her away.

They went into the banquet hall where a full bar was set up. Martin ordered a bourbon and water for himself and plain soda with a twist for Diana.

"Thanks," she murmured, after taking a sip. "I owe you one."

"You owe me more than one," he teased, before adding more gently, "You and L.C. aren't going to keep his condition a secret forever. Actually, I'm surprised more people don't know."

"Forever isn't an option. Anyway, L.C.'s calling the shots on this one. But I appreciate the concern," she added, sighing. She looped her arm through his and nodded toward the tables set for dinner. "Let's grab a seat near the dance floor. I've got my dancing shoes on tonight."

Though he gave the hand on his arm a compassionate squeeze, he played along, his groan dramatic. "Give me strength."

A few hours later, Adam stood on the terrace outside the banquet room and watched the couple returning from their stroll through the gardens. He'd kept an eye on Diana throughout the evening, determined to corner her at the most opportune moment. Now he had her. She wasn't going to avoid him this time, he vowed.

In the moonlight her pale blond hair, drawn into a black bow, glowed like a beacon. Her lyrical laughter floated toward him, carried by the faintest breeze. He compressed his lips into a harder line. Prescott was obviously in rare form tonight. He really had nothing against the younger man—other than thinking him a fool for venturing out of his league. Diana Fontaine was a dangerous woman—beautiful, vivacious and intelligent. A woman with those kinds of assets could manipulate almost any man she wanted to. He hoped for Prescott's sake that he hadn't already lost his heart to her; but then, every man had to learn his own lessons his own way.

As they approached the stairs, they were once again caught in the brighter illumination of the surrounding gas lamps. Adam stepped out from the shadow of one of the life-size marble angels that lined the terrace. It was Diana who spotted him. She froze midway up the stairs. Startled? He found it difficult to believe unless it was part of an act to trigger Prescott's protective instincts. Either way, she recovered quickly and lifted a deceptively delicate brow in mocking inquiry.

"How appropriate, Adam. I often think of fallen archangels when I look at you." She glanced over her shoulder to consider the view he'd had. "Taking up voyeurism?"

"I want to talk to you."

"He'd prefer having my head on a silver platter," she interpreted for Martin, "but we've become so depressingly civilized in this day and age."

"Diana," Martin warned, catching the dangerous narrowing of Adam's eyes.

"Oh, it's all right. Our district attorney has decided I need a lecture—again—and we might as well humor him." She patted Martin's hand and gave him a reassuring smile. "Go on inside. I'll join you in a minute."

Adam watched until Martin closed the French doors behind him, waiting until Diana stepped closer. In the soft light her hair and fair skin took on an ethereal glow, the bones of her oval face appeared more fragile; however, he knew better than to be duped by impressions of femininity. If the lady had any fear in her, he hadn't seen it yet, and if she had any weakness, it was only that she didn't know when to stop pushing.

"Why didn't you return my calls?" he demanded. Time was something he'd always felt a shortage of and had learned when not to waste it on senseless ceremony.

With the grace of a model, Diana leaned her hip against the stone balustrade and tapped her flat evening bag against the palm of her hand. "Well, I thought about it, but you don't exactly have a history of being nice to me on the phone, and what with court earlier in the day and appointments in the afternoon..."

"You decided to let me steam."

"You don't look any the worse for wear."

"I'm not about to give you the satisfaction of seeing me lose it in front of a couple of hundred witnesses."

Resigned to the realization that they were doomed to repeat the same tiresome arguments, she sighed and shook her head in regret. "Adam. When are you going to understand I'm not out to get you or your people. I'm simply doing my job."

"That's rich." He wouldn't allow himself to be taken in by the sincerity he saw warming those gray eyes, eyes that should have been green because their almond shape gave her the look of a feline. Instead they were a smoky gray, irritably changeable, in keeping with the consummate actress he believed she was. "You consider putting criminals like Madera back on the street your job?"

"When they're innocent, yes."

"He's guilty, just as he was guilty three years ago when he first went up on robbery charges."

"I'm not questioning his guilt *then*. I know he did it."

"Only because it's documented that he literally ran into the arresting officer with a knife in one hand and the money in the other. Thanks so much for the benevolent concession, Counselor."

Diana refused to be baited. "Calm down before smoke starts coming out of those flaring nostrils," she soothed. "Can't you accept that he might be one of the rehabilitated ones?"

"No. And don't tell me doing all that laundry in the pen made him see the error of his ways, or that his parole officer is the father figure to replace the one he didn't have as a kid. I've heard every story every bleeding heart like you could dream up."

"I wasn't about to give you a story—only the facts," she said patiently. "And it has nothing to do with his time in Huntsville or his relationship with his parole officer. He simply found something, *someone*, who gave him a reason to change. He fell in love."

Adam's smile mirrored pure sarcasm. "Great. You use that one in your opening remarks and this will be a nice short trial."

"I believe he'll be released by the time he comes up for arraignment, myself."

"Dream on. And be prepared to get yourself laughed out of court. Love." He muttered a crude expletive.

Calmly, Diana lifted an eyebrow, though inside, her own temper heated several degrees. It was at times like this when she began to wonder why she ever bothered with the man. "That's a difficult concept for you, I know. If you ever defrost long enough to have a meaningful relationship, you'll appreciate what a motivator it can be.

"Yes, love, Adam, and I won't be ashamed to use it because that's what happened. Carlos met a blue-eyed, blond nurse named Janie Allison and fell madly in love with her. He knew he didn't have the skills he needed to get a decent job to support a family, so he took a job as an all-night counter clerk in order to be able to afford the tuition to go to auto mechanics school during the day. Is that something your people managed to get on record?"

"Our files don't exactly read like novels, but do go on. I don't mind you digging your own hole."

"He graduates next month, which is a good thing, because as you should also know, Janie has discovered she's pregnant and they'll need the extra income his new job will provide."

Adam folded his arms across his chest. "I don't suppose you can see how that creates the motive for committing the alleged crime?"

"Feasible, but in this case wrong; however I *am* grateful you deigned to use the term *alleged*. Aren't you listening to me? He wasn't about to take that kind of risk. He knew Janie wouldn't stand for it if she found out."

"But the burglary occurred a half block from their apartment," he reminded her.

"He's not the only person capable of having committed it. Come on, we both know that's not the best of neighborhoods."

"We also have an eyewitness who identified Madera in the lineup."

Diana dismissed that with a toss of her head. "The man's a classic bigot, and I'll expose him as such if you put him on the witness stand. On the other hand, my client has an irrefutable alibi: he was with Father Lopez at Saint Anthony's that night before going to work."

"Agreed, but there's a half hour he can't account for between the time he left the church and the time he showed up at his job. The burglarized house is almost midway between those two points, and it's only a ten-minute walk from point A to point B. That left him with twenty unaccountable minutes."

"*If* he had walked, which he didn't. It was raining and he took the bus, even though it takes a longer route."

"But we haven't been able to locate anyone who remembers seeing him, not even the bus driver. Your client's guilty."

"Oh, please." She began to turn away, disgusted, then spun back again. "You have no fingerprints, no evidence was found either on Madera or at his residence, nothing except the questionable testimony of someone who admits all Hispanics look alike to him and the victim's irrelevant comment that he and Carlos didn't like each other. In the meantime my client and his wife have been exposed to classic examples of prejudice by a couple of cops who give the rest of the police force a bad name. No, save it," she interrupted when he began to protest. "I know what story they gave to cover themselves. I happen to find it highly implausible that Carlos managed to get that kind of bruise by tripping and hitting his head—even against a brick wall. Also, we both know it was that 'legal' search of their home that made Janie end up being hospitalized, and so help me, Adam, if she loses that baby, I'll have those officers' badges."

He had the grace to look away. He had to admit she had got him there. Those two officers had really pushed things to the limit. "I spoke with her doctor myself before coming here this evening. He's confident she'll go full term."

"Lovely. Now all she has to deal with is the prospect of raising her child alone while her husband does time for a crime he didn't commit." She'd been surprised and pleased that he possessed the compassion to check on Janie, but he was still a stubborn mule about the rest. "If you want some advice, I'd look for a graceful way out of this one, because you're going to land up with egg on your face."

"Nice try, but forget it. My sympathy for Mrs. Madera isn't going to change my mind. You're the one who should heed a little advice." He let his gaze drift over her. "Ever since you came back to town, you've made a big show of being the poor man's champion, but this time you're tilting at windmills. If you defend Madera, you're going to find yourself being judged as guilty as he is."

"This from the man who would probably reinstate witch-hunting if he thought he could get away with it," she replied dryly.

"I know who I'd go after first," he snapped.

Diana's laugh was taunting. "You're a marvel. Why don't you admit it's me and the fact that my last name is Fontaine that makes you see red."

He was tempted to wrap his fingers around her slender neck. It infuriated him that she stood there and not only mocked him, but made herself look victimized. "I'm trying to help keep the crime statistics down from epidemic proportions," he ground out, "and the last thing I need in my life is some hotshot lawyer with a guilt complex coming back to town and tossing around her services gratis like a Neiman-Marcus rendition of Joan of Arc."

"What!"

"You heard me. Do you think I'm blind?"

Diana's breasts rose and fell with every agitated breath she took. Her eyes began to shoot off the same white-hot sparks his did. "Blind, deaf and about as dumb as anyone can get! Why you—*oaf*—you think I bust my butt for free out of guilt?"

"Of one form or another."

"What's *that* supposed to mean?"

"Maybe I'm not sure what's behind all these gestures of charity, but I promise you I'm going to find out."

Diana crossed the few steps between them and angrily jabbed a finger against his chest. "You wouldn't recognize the truth if you tripped over it in broad daylight. The day's going to come—"

"For heaven's sake, will you two knock it off before you have everyone inside standing by the windows!"

Neither one of them had seen or heard Martin come out. He stepped between them, as if expecting the worse to happen.

It was Adam who took the first step backward, yet power and anger emanated from him with every deep breath. His icy glare never strayed from Diana. "Your call, Counselor. If I were you, I'd think twice this time. Your luck's not going to hold."

She lifted her chin. "Luck doesn't have anything to do with it."

Something should have cracked, his face went that rigid. Without another word he spun on his heel and strode away. Diana closed her eyes. Never in her life had she been moved to experience such violence. She could actually feel her hands trembling from her suppressed emotions.

Martin considered her for a moment before raising the drink he was carrying to his lips. "One of these days you're going to push him too far," he predicted.

She cast him a sidelong look. The hint of a sparkle returned to her eyes. "Don't be ridiculous. The man's absolutely mad about me."

The bourbon lodged midway down Martin's throat. He made a strangled sound and went into a coughing fit. "Right," he wheezed, wiping tears from his eyes. "Just remember Othello was mad about Desdemona, too, and look what happened to her."

Three

———

Miss Fontaine..."

"Diana, will you give us a statement?"

The small swarm of reporters and TV cameramen surrounded her the moment she stepped from the elevator into the courthouse lobby. Her smile remained congenial, while inside she was relieved she'd convinced Carlos and Janie to take the other elevator down to the garage where she had someone waiting to drive them home.

It was over. They'd won without the case having come to trial. Eventually the fatigue that was a result of forty-eight hours of frantic work would catch up with her, but for the moment, relief and intense satisfaction prevailed.

She stopped in the middle of the lobby, with the group following like a colony of bees. She was on friendly terms with a few of them, though never believed for a moment that friendship was what brought them here. She'd produced a good story, raised the interest of the public. For the moment she was hot. Tomorrow it could be a herd of cattle loose on the interstate. That knowledge kept her from taking it all too seriously.

"Where'd you stash the Maderas, Diana?"

Diana's smile widened, despite the microphones inching closer to her face. "My client and his wife decided they'd like to celebrate his release privately. I assured them you wouldn't mind."

There were a few chuckles and fewer grumbles from disappointed reporters who realized there would be more legwork to do before meeting their deadline. Then, as if reacting to an invisible signal, everyone got down to business.

"Were you always aware there was another witness who could prove Carlos Madera innocent?"

"Definitely," Diana replied, inclining her head. "There were several people on the bus with him. It was our hope someone would see our televised appeal last night and come forward on his behalf before today's arraignment. When it turned out to be a retired member of the Corpus Christi police force, we felt it was twice the vindication. We're extremely grateful to Mr. DeMott."

"What about your charges against the arresting officers?"

"We've been assured the police department is operating an internal investigation. We're satisfied."

"What's next on the agenda, Diana?"

"A full night's sleep for a change—I hope." After another round of polite laughter, Diana went on to mention the charity bazaar she was cochairing, the benefits of which would go to several groups in the city. She knew it wasn't what they wanted to hear, but she wasn't about to risk losing a potential juror for a trial because they'd heard about an upcoming case from her.

"You've proved the district attorney's office wrong again," another reporter injected, not yet satisfied with what she'd given them. "This latest victory isn't going to endear you to Adam Rhodes, is it?"

She was about to respond to that when the subject of their curiosity entered the lobby himself. He was wearing a dove-gray pin-striped suit, and even though it was only April, his tan was already dark, contrasting attractively against his crisp white shirt. They hadn't seen each other since the night at the country club, and she was a little surprised at the intensity of the rush of excitement that sped through her. Collecting herself, she indicated his arrival with a nod of her head and suggested the reporter get himself a direct opinion.

It would have been impossible for Adam to have missed spotting the group across the lobby, but it disturbed him how quickly his gaze zeroed in on Diana. She looked like a queen holding court, calm and assured. Her hair was drawn back, probably knotted in one of those sleek, elegant chignons she was so talented at creating. He'd never seen it loose when she was working, and was sure she was aware of what a distraction it would be. The severely tailored suits many professional women wore were not for her. The pink with black-trim ensemble had the classic yet soft lines of a Chanel suit, and accenting its femininity, she wore those trademark pearls of hers.

He'd been told about the witness who'd walked into the courtroom during Madera's arraignment while on his way back here. He could see it mirrored now in

Diana's face—the elation, as well as the fatigue and relief. Whatever their personal differences, professionally he understood how hard she'd worked on behalf of
her client. It made it easier for him, when he reached
her, to extend his hand in congratulations.

"Mr. Rhodes, what's your opinion of the outcome of
this trial?"

Because he was caught off guard by the surprising
discovery of how delicate the bones of her hand really
were, and how soft her skin, he almost missed the
question. He covered it by murmuring something appropriate to her before turning to the reporter.

"Justice prevailed, Jim."

"Then you believe Carlos Madera is innocent?"

"It would be foolish not to."

"Yet your office was sure he was guilty," a female
reporter reminded him.

"Based on the evidence and testimony we had at the
time." He shrugged, playing down the formerly ag-
gressive stance though, inside, his emotions were closer
to seething. Heads were going to spin because of this,
starting with the police chief's and on downward. If he
couldn't get his people to do their job, how was the
D.A.'s office supposed to maintain credibility?

"What do you think of Ms. Fontaine's tactic of putting her client's picture on television and pleading for
the public's assistance?" someone else called out.

Now they were beginning to skate onto thin ice, he
thought, swinging his gaze back to Diana. She lifted an
eyebrow, indicating her own curiosity. Amusement accented the upward slant of her eyes. He dropped his
gaze to her mouth and wondered fleetingly if she were
aware her lipstick had worn off, leaving it looking de-

cidedly vulnerable. Out of necessity, he tore his gaze away.

"I'm never surprised at anything Ms. Fontaine does; however, if I were in need of a good defense attorney, I'd want one who would be as tenacious as she is."

"That sounds conciliatory. Does this mean the cold war between the two of you is over?"

"I think you have what you need for your stories. Now, if you'll excuse me..." He reached over and took hold of a surprised Diana's elbow. "May I have a word with you?"

There were several protests, but Adam ignored them and led her into an elevator that had just emptied. After he'd quickly punched the button to the floor where his office was located, the doors slid closed.

The silence was acute after the challenge of listening to reporters yell in competition to be heard, and it emphasized their awareness of each other. But like Adam, Diana stared up at the floor numbers, watching as they lit progressively.

Now what? she wondered. She'd done nothing he could take exception to, yet there was something going on in that head of his.

"Just for the record," she murmured, unable to resist the urge, "if you ever *did* call me for counsel, I wouldn't take your case for free."

"Just for the record, I wouldn't offer it to you in the first place."

"Now I recognize you," she drawled, tongue in cheek. "For a minute there, you had me believing that performance downstairs."

As the doors slid open, he sent her a dark look, then motioned for her to precede him. He didn't need the cute remarks any more than he needed her flirting with him. He would have thought a woman with her physical assets could find more than enough companions to practice on. He might not be immune to her, but he didn't need her complicating the situation and clouding his priorities.

"What are you doing here?"

Adam transferred his glare to Muriel. Leave it to her to clear his head. "Last time I looked, that was still my name on the door," he muttered, picking up his messages from the corner of her desk.

"But you're not due back until..." Her voice drifted off as she kept staring at Diana. "Oh, my—you're her!"

Not about to let a potential ally slip through her fingers, especially in this dubious place, Diana extended her hand. "I see my reputation precedes me."

"I'm Muriel Littlejohn. I have to tell you I think you were wonderful on TV."

"Why, thank you."

"My sister and I sat there the rest of the evening trying to decide who it was you reminded us of. You don't watch any of the nighttime soaps, do you?"

"Well, no."

"Then you wouldn't know who we were talking about, anyway. But we think the service you're providing people down on their luck and abused by the system is the nicest thing. I, for one, never did believe that Carlo fellow was guilty."

Having heard more than enough, Adam turned away. "I'll be in my office. Let me know when you two are finished."

"I'd better go in, too," Diana said, making a move to follow. "It was very nice meeting you, Muriel."

"Wait! Would you like some coffee? Tea? No? Well, I'll be here if you need anything at all." Glancing toward Adam's office to make sure he'd had sufficient time to move out of earshot, she leaned farther across her desk. Papers shifted under her ample bosom. "I just wanted to tell you—don't feel pressured into closing the door. I never do, myself."

"Thanks. I'll play it by ear."

When Adam heard Diana finally come in, he turned to find her slumped against the shut door. She had her fingers pressed to her lips and she was either shivering from cold—which was unlikely since the air-conditioning had yet to be turned on—or laughing. He shoved his hands into his pants pockets, leaned back against his desk and sighed.

"I'm glad you're amused."

"Wait—wait. Give me a minute." She took several deep breaths before regaining her composure. Finally she dabbed the tears from her eyes with the backs of her index fingers. "I suppose every office has one. Ours is equally precious."

"That's not exactly the word I'd use to describe Muriel."

"No? I can have the most frustrating day and in five minutes Oscar can reduce all the world's problems down to a gross of missing pencils."

Oscar sounded more to his liking. Reluctantly, one corner of Adam's mouth curved upward. "Is there a secret to coping?"

"Agree, flatter and generally confound whenever you can. Staying out of the office is easier, though. I like you a lot more when you smile."

She set down her briefcase and was strolling around his office before he realized what she'd said. The pleasure the casual admission gave him had him eyeing her warily. "Is that an example?"

"An example of what?" she asked vaguely. His office was just as she'd pictured it: formal, with little to differentiate it from any of the other offices in the building, except perhaps for its size and the quality of its furnishings.

"Of being flattering and generally confounding."

Picking up a carved wood duck from a bookshelf, she ran her fingertips over its smooth surface and smiled. "What a suspicious character you are." She replaced the piece and moved on to another shelf where several golf trophies were given prominence. "I didn't realize you were this good. Did you ever consider turning pro?"

"Once—for maybe twenty minutes. I soon realized it wouldn't be enough."

She nodded and moved on. He was too intense not to want to effect a change in people, in the system. At least they had that in common. At the window she glanced out over the city. It had grown since she'd left. Oddly enough, though she'd experienced a relatively happy childhood here, she hadn't regretted leaving. She'd needed the time away.

"It's not quite Boston, is it?" Adam observed, watching her.

"No, but then again it's home. You have a better view than me. Through my window you get a panoramic view of the accounting firm of Waters, Bakersfield, Cleary and Johnson, and miles of calculator paper spilling over desks and across the floor. The only incentive I have to look out the window is to see if it's taken over the office yet. Someone needs to write a thriller about it. I'll bet there's more than one accoun-

tant who's had nightmares about the stuff winding itself up around their legs and then tying them to their
chairs...."

Adam ran a smoothing hand over his nape and
cleared his throat. "I've never read that type of book
myself."

"No? What do you read?"

"What is this, twenty questions?"

"I was only trying to make polite conversation, or
rather see if it's possible. You know chronologically
we've known each other for a long time, but we've never
chatted like this before."

He frowned at her as she crossed before him to go to
inspect the other side of the room. "I didn't ask you up
here for a chat."

"You didn't *ask*." She paused by a black lacquered
chest. "Oh, this is lovely," she murmured, opening the
double swing doors.

"By all means help yourself," Adam invited sarcastically.

Diana admired the glass-and-mirror interior, the
crystal glasses and decanters, but shook her head. "No,
thanks. I rarely drink. Hate the taste, but can I pour you
a Scotch?"

"No, thank you."

He set his teeth. She was good, he had to give her
that. Some people wouldn't want you to know they'd
made a study of you; she did, knowing honesty created
its own leverage. He let his gaze slide down over her as
she bent again to shut the doors.

"'Know thy enemy....' Is that it?" he drawled.

"I know you won't believe me, but I don't consider
you the enemy, Adam. A fascinating study, yes, but not

the enemy." She came to stand before him and they faced each other squarely. "Why am I up here?"

Gone was the teasing banter; the dry wit was cast off like a shed skin. Here was the Diana Fontaine the rest of the world got to see, but which she usually kept hidden from him. Her eyes were softened by appeal, and seemed to him a little sad. Her mouth, accented by the faint cleft in her chin, appeared almost tremulous. When she behaved like a she-cat who enjoyed flexing her claws in his hide and his ego, he found it less difficult to ignore her other charms; but now, like this—damn her, she made him wonder.

"I wanted to congratulate you."

"You more or less did that downstairs."

"All right, so I also feel I owe you an apology. I was wrong and you were right. There. Satisfied?" Disgruntled, and needing to get away from those searching gray eyes, he sidestepped her and moved around his desk to look out the window himself.

Diana considered his rigid, broad back before demurely dropping her gaze back down to her folded hands. "I suppose I'd better be. If you get any more sincere, you'll burst a vein."

"Do you ever let up?" he snapped.

"I'm sorry, you're right. I do have a tendency to needle you. But you must understand, it's only because I find it frustrating that we can't communicate like two professional people should."

He let out a long breath and turned around. "That's the other reason I wanted to talk to you. The remark about our cold war that that reporter made downstairs expressed the situation perfectly. We've got to find a middle ground on which to deal with each other before we become a comic strip on the editorial page of the morning paper."

"I agree, and—I might add—it's about time."

"Besides," he continued, sitting down in his desk chair and folding his hands across his stomach, "all that undermines the seriousness of the work we do."

Diana perched herself on the corner of his desk and crossed her legs. Flicking away a tuft of lint from her skirt, she missed Adam's disapproving glance. "We could hold a joint press conference under the guise of announcing a program designed to clear up the backlog of court cases. You could say something to the effect that you were instigating a new program and would be meeting with a number of other attorneys, as well."

"Forget it. Since we already do something like that, they'd see right through it and accuse us of staging."

"Well then, you come up with a better idea." She shrugged, her attention caught by a picture frame near her right hand. She picked it up and saw it was a photograph of a woman several years younger than herself, holding a dark-haired little boy who shared the same laughing green eyes. Was this the blonde Martin had mentioned? "Pretty lady," she murmured. "But I don't see a family resemblance."

"Do you mind?" He reached out and straightened the picture after she replaced it. Her habit of touching things was beginning to get to him; that she never put anything back precisely as it had been made it all the worse. It was intentional, he was sure of it, knowing he would be forced to think about her even after she was gone, whenever he straightened something. "You may not have anything else to do today other than resting on your laurels, but I do."

"All right." She sighed, lacing her fingers in her lap. "You've got my undivided attention. Shoot."

"Don't tempt me." He picked up a pencil and drew it through his fingers. "I think what happened downstairs today was a good start," he continued, getting them back on track. "I think for the most part our actions should speak for us. In the future when we meet at a function, I'll make a point of exchanging a few words with you."

"You usually do."

"And you'll can the one-liners."

"Adam, I'm crushed. You enjoy my wit; you're just too stubborn to admit it. Okay—okay," she added, upon seeing his mouth tighten. "I'll try to lighten up a bit."

"You'll understand if I don't hold my breath. In the meantime you could refrain from taking on all that gratis work just because you know it irritates me. The media loves it when I call something black and you show up the next day calling it white."

Diana closed her eyes and visualized herself dumping a bowl of spaghetti sauce over his head, hoping it would help her keep from saying something she might later regret. "I should have known. This isn't about a truce or working out our differences. You want total capitulation!"

"Not at all. I'm perfectly willing to negotiate on certain cases."

"Didn't this situation with Madera prove anything to you? The innocent shouldn't have to *negotiate* for their freedom, and I don't take a case unless I'm convinced of the accused's innocence."

"It must feel wonderful being right all the time."

"Well, you should know!" Diana made a soft, almost pained sound and pressed her fingers to her forehead. "Will you listen to us? This has nothing to do with being right or wrong. It has to do with a Rhodes worrying that a Fontaine is getting the upper hand again." She slid off the desk and paced back and forth across his office, her clasped hands tucked under her chin. Finally she came back and, resting her palms flat on the desk, leaned toward him. "Adam, you can be a slave to that sad, old feud our parents started, but leave me out of it. In that respect, I'm no threat to you."

"If you meant that, then why did you come back?"

"I came back.... I can't tell you why I came back," she murmured. She searched his pale blue eyes, had a flash image of the child he'd been, and felt an empathy for the hurt and confusion he must have experienced all those years ago. He'd been six when the scandal broke; his brother, James, nine. She'd been luckier in that sense; she wasn't born until months later.

"Why can't you let the past go?" she asked quietly. "As far as L.C. is concerned, it ended when your father died. He has no argument with you. He admires you."

Adam's laugh was bitter, and he shook his head, pushing himself out of the chair to stride over to the window. "You spin a better line than he does. My father was right when he warned me about letting my guard down with a Fontaine."

"Justin was a bitter, hardened man by then, and he bent the truth to hide his own inadequacies. James realized that; it's why he ran away."

A muscle jerked spasmodically in Adam's cheek. "Leave my brother out of this."

Diana bowed her head, realizing that the loss still hurt him deeply. James had been killed in a motorcycle accident only months after leaving home. "All right, but I'll ask you for the same courtesy. Leave me out of your anger. I can understand having these disagreements with you based on the principles and technicalities of a case, but I will not be condemned for taking one on simply because I'm my father's daughter."

"Do you deny you provoke me, that you instigated many of those skirmishes we've had?"

The hint of a smile played around her mouth. "Adam, I'm only human. I'll admit you bring out a streak of mischievousness in me, but you must see that I often taunt you only because I can't believe in the absurdity of the situation. Some people throw tantrums, I try to offset things with humor. Almost everyone holds with the theory that tragedy is the basis for most comedy."

"I fail to see the humor in a man having an affair with his best friend's wife."

"No, that wasn't funny," she whispered. "Nor was that smear campaign Justin started to try to get L.C. disbarred, or any of the other cruel things they did to each other to get revenge. But all that concerned our parents, not us. If you want to do battle with me, you're going to have to come up with a better reason than the one you're harboring. I only hope you'll see how senseless that is and let us start over. Our politics might be different, but I don't think our basic ideals are far apart."

Adam stared at her over his shoulder. "Am I hearing this correctly? You want us to be friends?"

"Is that such an inconceivable idea?"

"You tell me. I ask you one simple question about why you came back to Texas and you can't be honest enough to tell me. It seems to me a friendship needs to have a foundation of trust if it's expected to grow. You're not showing me any, so why should I play the fool and believe you?"

"My God," Diana whispered. "Justin did a job on you. When we were young and we ran into each other, it used to hurt my feelings to have you walk around me as if I had some kind of contagious disease. L.C. would try to comfort me by telling me to give it time. He'd say given time and some distance from your father's influence, all that ice you'd enclosed your feelings in would thaw. But he was wrong. You're cold through and through."

Adam stepped closer and leaned against one of the leather chairs facing his desk. "I get it now. You were called back here as bait. L.C. heard the talk about running me for state office in the next election. He lobbied against me for *this* job and didn't succeed, so he's called home his secret weapon. Just how far was he willing to go? If you didn't succeed in making me look incompetent, was he willing to let you try to blackmail me in the bedroom?"

Diana swung at him, but his reflexes were faster. He grabbed her wrist, then pulled her against him. Fury seethed between them, obliterating the hold of his fingers.

"You wish," she seethed, tossing back her head to glare up at him. "That would make it easier for you to handle the guilt, wouldn't it?"

"What the hell are you talking about?"

"You want me." She saw the flicker deep in his eyes and knew she'd scored a direct hit. "Yes, I can see it,

and sense it. A woman always knows when a man's interested in her. Unfortunately, I'm the wrong woman.
It disturbs you to think that lightning can strike twice,
doesn't it? You don't want to believe you can want me
the same way your mother wanted my father."

Adam knew he was an inch away from doing something drastic and should put her away from him; he
knew that he was sealing his own fate by not listening to
his instincts, but she was right: he wanted her, and having it a spoken thing between them made desire flare all
the more quickly, blocking out everything except need.

"You're damned sure of yourself," he said, knowing how it would provoke and cancel any retreat for
either of them.

"I'm sure of both of us," she whispered, and pressed
her lips to his.

Too late, she realized her folly. He was ready for her.
They'd been ready for each other for a long time. Passion needed no coaxing to stoke it into a full, blazing
heat. As their lips parted to each other's, their bodies
came together like two adversaries who had studied
each other to the core—knew every strength, every
weakness—and intended to use it all to bring the other
to their knees. Yet there could be no winner, she realized, arching closer under the pressure of the hand that
scorched down her back, not in a moment this volcanic. They both would pay.

Adam forgot time and place, knew only that she fit
against his body as if she'd been born for him. Her re-
sponsiveness made him ache for more, even while he
sated himself with her rich taste and elusive scent. She
was softer than he'd imagined, and so incredibly slender. Despite her delicateness, she could lead him into the
burning furnace of hell and he knew he would follow

willingly. The truth hit him straight on; he felt the pain and gasped for air.

The ringing phone was a shrill harbinger of reality breaking them apart. For an instant they stared at each other in an odd mixture of need and disbelief before Adam spun around and grabbed blindly for the phone.

"What!" His voice sounded raw to his own ears, as strained as his breathing. He listened, struggling to control both. "I'll tell her," he muttered a moment later, and hung up.

But when he turned around, she was gone. His gaze shot from the half-open door to the empty chair where her briefcase had been, and back again. Gone, as if she'd never been there. Only the belly-deep ache and the dampness causing his shirt to stick to his back proved otherwise.

He sat down on the edge of his desk.

For the better part of thirty-nine years he'd been a loner, had prided himself on that. His father had instilled strong lessons in him to look to himself. To satisfy his needs, not to rely on anyone, not to need anyone but himself... And now there was Diana. He rubbed his hands over his face and barely stifled a groan. The old man had been right: L. C. Fontaine played dirty.

As he drew in a deep breath, he caught a lingering hint of her perfume in the air; and he cursed the old reprobate—even as he had to admire his style.

Four

During her ride down the elevator, Diana ran a hand over her hair, her suit and called herself a few choice variations on words for a fool. In less than sixty seconds, by allowing her sexuality to interfere with her work, she'd undone a half decade's worth of progress that professional women like herself had been striving for.

"Oh, hang progress," she muttered under her breath a moment later. She had wanted to kiss him, and so she had. If that wasn't being liberated, she didn't know what was. It wasn't as if he hadn't kissed her back, she thought, a whimsical smile playing around her mouth.

But as quickly as it came, the smile vanished, logic prevailing. If he'd been a bear before, he was going to be a dragon now, especially if Muriel Littlejohn got a peek at him before he'd had a chance to recomb his hair.

What *had* the woman said to her when she'd dashed by her desk?

At the lobby, the elevator came to a halt and Diana stepped from carpeting to marble, while scanning the corridor for a sign of lingering reporters. In the process, her gaze flicked over a woman in a white, nurse-style uniform walking toward her. Then she did a double take.

"Rosie...." As fast as her mind registered the distress she saw in her housekeeper's wide-planed face, she felt a knot of tension form in her stomach. "It's not Dad?"

"No, no." Upon reaching her, Rose Warren enclosed Diana's outstretched hand within both of hers. "I told them not to upset you. Didn't they...? Mercy, child. Let me catch my breath."

"You're shaking, and as cold as ice," Diana said, her concern shifting to the woman who, in many ways, had replaced the mother she'd lost. "Here. Sit down and tell me what's wrong."

"It's Leon. He's been arrested, along with two other boys from that gang I told you he was running around with. They were caught stealing a typewriter and radio from the Methodist church near the house. *A church.*" She lifted the crumpled handkerchief in her hand to her lips, and, keening softly, began rocking back and forth. "I raised five good children, but this one... I told Leon, he was going to put me in an early grave. Just last week I told him."

Diana placed a comforting arm around her and hugged her. "Stop that this minute. How are you going to box his ears if you make yourself sick and have to go into the hospital?"

"Humph. He's too big for any of that, anyhow. Too big and too wild."

Diana felt her heart contract in compassion. She knew the older woman was partially right; Leon was six foot five and still growing. He was hardly recognizable from the chubby little doe-eyed boy she used to love to carry when she'd been barely more than a child herself. But wild? Maybe a bit spoiled, because his mother had made the mistake of making things too easy for him, but she dreaded thinking he was out of control.

She dropped her gaze to the larger hand clasping her own. The contrast between them was more than a difference in pigmentation. Rose's hands were rough from years of hard work; Diana's were soft, treated occasionally to a professional manicure. She understood Rose's dreams of creating a better life for her children than she'd had, but she'd backed those dreams with strict discipline. Of the six, two daughters were schoolteachers, two more were nurses and the only other boy besides Leon was opening his own electrical contracting business. Now in her late fifties, she lacked either the strength or heart to be the disciplinarian with the most challenging of her offspring.

"I'll go to the police station and take care of things," Diana told her. "You go home and lie down." She hadn't noticed before, but there were dark rings beginning to show beneath the other woman's eyes.

"I can't do that. I left the ironing board in the middle of the kitchen, and there's one of those chicken casseroles you like so much starting to bake in the oven. I think I remembered to lower the heat. Oh, Lord, I don't know. When I got the call from the police station, I just lost all my good sense."

"Forget the casserole. Forget the ironing. How did you get here? Did you drive?" When Rose nodded, Diana rose and drew her to her feet. "Fine. Now drive yourself home. As soon as I can get Leon out, I'll bring him over."

"Bless you. I hated having to come disturb you like this, but I didn't know what else to do."

"You did the right thing. Now go."

As soon as she was certain Rose was on her way, Diana glanced at her watch, then headed for the row of phones at the other side of the lobby. She dug a coin out of the side compartment of her briefcase, dropped it into an unoccupied phone, and punched in a series of numbers.

"Andy, it's me," she said, upon being put through to her secretary. "Hope you're in the mood to do some rescheduling and then run over to my house. It's going to be another of those days."

It was past six that evening when Diana finally pulled into the circular driveway of the house she'd been born in. She'd almost forgotten that since her return to Texas, Wednesday had been the day she set aside to dine quietly with her father.

She switched off the engine of her Cadillac and took a moment to simply sit and catch her breath. In the amber glow of sunset, the two-story mansion looked like a beloved photograph yellowed with age. Guarding the front door sat the two stone lions she used to climb all over during the stage when she'd been certain she simply *had* to grow up and become a cowgirl. The juniper and ligustrum hedges were almost grown together now, but once they'd provided the secret maze for when she'd worked undercover as a government spy.

So many happy memories, she mused, and yet when she returned to Texas, she'd been adamant about getting her own place to live. Her independence was important to her. But most of all, she couldn't bear to stay here day in and day out and watch an era disintegrate. That was the truth she couldn't bring herself to admit to her father. She wasn't that strong.

The front door opened and Walters, her father's houseman, bent—as much as his rigid bearing allowed—to peer at her through the windshield. He'd replaced Rose, who'd left after Diana went away to college complaining there was no longer enough work for her. Diana found the man's devotion to formality wearing, but since L.C. thought it enormously entertaining, she suffered through it. Lately her father had taken to calling him "the General," and she suspected Walters was not at all displeased.

Her moment of quiet reflection interrupted, she got out of the car and climbed the half-dozen low steps to where the Englishman patiently waited. "Hello, Walters. Sorry to keep you waiting. I thought the cat sleeping under the hood of the car had caught itself in the fan belt, but I'm sure I'm mistaken," she said deadpan, coming up with the most absurd comment she could think of.

"Yes, miss. Your father is expecting you in the study."

One of these days, she thought, passing him and entering the cooler foyer, one of these days she was going to figure out something to say that would ruffle those starched feathers.

She laid down her briefcase on the chair beneath the brass hat rack and went to locate her father. The scent of rose potpourri still lingered in the air. It had been a

favorite of her mother's, and along with an old photo
album in the living room, it was the only reminder of
the woman who had died shortly after giving birth to
her only child.

"There you are. I was beginning to think I'd been
stood up."

Diana grinned at the long-legged man who eagerly
tossed away the newspaper he'd been reading the moment she entered the study. Dressed in a navy blue and
salmon striped polo shirt and navy blue slacks, he
looked like he'd just come off a golf course. His thick
mane of hair was snow-white, his tan deeper than
Adam's, and in the distinguished, sculpted lines of his
face, she saw herself forty years from now. Seeing him
like this, looking fit, with a sparkle in his gray eyes that
were just a shade darker than her own, she found it impossible to believe that he was ill.

"I *did* have a better offer," she drawled, on impulse
adding a hug to the kiss she gave him. "But halfway to
the restaurant, my conscience got the best of me, so I
dumped him."

"Brat." He chuckled. Then, as he studied her more
closely, he drew his heavy white eyebrows together in a
frown. "Uh-oh. What's wrong?"

Diana rolled her eyes. "How do you do that? In court
they say I have a poker face, but you can read me like a
book."

"Try becoming a parent and find out."

In response, she wrinkled her nose at him and withdrew to the bar. "I would, if I could get around the little technicality you imposed about wanting me to
provide you with a son-in-law first. Can I pour you a
bourbon?"

"Is the desert dry? The way you and the General ration me these days, it's a wonder I'm allowed anything at all. And what's wrong with my wanting you to be settled down with a family of your own?"

"Nothing," she conceded, on a sigh. "But I haven't exactly been overrun with marriage proposals."

"Why not? You're a beautiful woman. What's wrong with men these days?"

Diana filled two tumblers with ice from a stainless-steel bucket, poured her father's drink, and then mineral water for herself. "A lot of them still can't handle the idea of having a wife who might be equally—if not more—successful than they are."

"What about that investment broker who was chasing you like a buck during rut? The one that sent you all those flowers while you were down here two Christmases ago."

"What a charming and appropriate analogy." She brought him his drink and settled with her own in the armchair facing his. "Unfortunately I discovered there was a Mrs. Buck."

L.C. made a deep grumbling sound, but wisely refrained from expounding, and took a sip of his drink. "Well, what is it that's got you looking like you've been walking all day with a burr in your shoe? I thought after getting that young Hispanic fellow released this morning, you'd be on top of the world." When she gave him an arch look, he shrugged. "Oscar came over with some papers I had to sign, so he filled me in. Besides, I'm still the senior member of the firm and I have a right to know what's going on."

"Did I say anything?"

"I'm just letting you know this old dinosaur isn't ready to be planted yet."

"Can't you just picture Saint Peter sighing with relief?"

He tried to repress a grin but failed. "All right. Out with it. What happened today?"

Diana sighed. "Leon was arrested."

"Rose's Leon? Good Lord.... Why?"

"He and two other boys broke into a church and were caught trying to steal some things from the minister's office."

"The poor woman must be devastated."

"She is. She's been having a difficult time with him for a while now. Ever since he started to run around with this gang of boys. Luckily he's still seventeen, and the minister was willing to let things slide since he got his equipment back. And I promised to get the boys counseling; but Leon turns eighteen in a few weeks, and if he pulls something like this again, there's a good chance that he'll go to jail. I'm not sure I've impressed upon him what that means, but I know it would destroy Rose."

L.C. shook his head, his expression grim but sympathetic. "Yes, I can imagine."

For a moment Diana continued swirling the ice cubes in her glass, but she could feel her father waiting for her to continue. "Oh, all right—something else happened today. I'm surprised you didn't see it on the evening news." She was certain it would make the morning paper, as well.

"Are you referring to that interesting little exchange you had with District Attorney Rhodes this morning?"

She sent him a mild look. "So it *did* make the early news."

"The lead story."

"And?"

"And what?"

"Don't play innocent with me, you old war horse. I'll tell you right now, it was all a performance. Oh, he believes in Carlos's innocence, but as for his professional pat on the back to me, that was all hype."

"A Rhodes is born with the instincts of a politician in his blood," L.C. reminded her.

"Ten minutes later he was accusing me of taking cases to irritate him."

"You *do* have a talent for bringing attention to a case that ordinarily wouldn't get picked up by the paper beyond a two-inch mention tucked away beside the supermarket ads."

"When I believe a client is getting a raw deal from the system, I *want* the media involved. The public needs to see when the system fails them."

"What are you going to do when, one of these days, you're proved wrong?"

Diana exhaled in frustration. "You're beginning to sound like *him*."

"Maybe he studied the Greek tragedies in school himself."

"How about sticking to reality and forgetting drama?"

"All right, but you still won't like it. The reality is that I agree with Adam if he's been warning you about the danger of sticking your neck out once too often. It's possible—mind you, I only said *possible*, not *proba-ble*—that somewhere down the line you might be taken in by someone's sad story. It's happened to all of us, my dear, and it's not something I'd care to see you go through. If the press has been along for the ride, they can turn on you in a second, then feed on your misfortune for days, like vultures on carrion. I've seen good attorneys—strong men—destroyed that way.''

Touched by the concern she felt emanating from him, Diana leaned forward to touch his knee. "Don't, Dad. You taught me better than you give yourself credit for.''

He gave her a smile that didn't quite remove the worry in his eyes. "Sometimes I think being the parent of a grown child is more difficult than being one of a youngster. There are so many things you remember you forgot to say; lessons to teach; mistakes to be corrected.''

"Do I feel a lecture coming on?'' she asked. Teasing, because she didn't like the way this conversation was heading. She'd never worn tinted glasses where L. C. Fontaine was concerned. She knew he was simply a man—better than most, but human, nonetheless. It was unbearable for her to think he could be having doubts now, at this critical stage in his life, about how he might have failed her.

Seeing the overbright smile on his only child's face, L.C. sighed. "No. No lecture. Isn't there something else you want to talk about? Something about you and Adam? Yes,'' he said, catching her stunned look. "I know. I've been watching it develop for years. I used to watch you watch him when you thought no one was looking. For a time it made me worry—I was almost relieved when you decided to do all your schooling in the East. You've both always been such charismatic people, even back then, and I knew you'd only end up being hurt if things developed too quickly.''

"I had no idea,'' she murmured, adding, "but you're mostly wrong. Oh, he's attracted to me all right, but his dislike that I'm a Fontaine is a strong antidote.''

"Something you rarely let him forget, eh?''

"I refuse to be treated like a strain of virus that needs to be quarantined."

"I hope you two come to terms with this before one of you kills the other," L.C. drawled, before taking another swallow of his drink.

Diana shook her head, more in confusion than annoyance. "I can't see how. He actually suggested that I was your puppet and that we were up to no good."

"Did he? Well, there's no telling what nonsense Justin filled his head with; when it came to protecting his own ego, Justin never could stand being second best." He finished his drink and set his empty glass down on the side table between them. "It's a shame. Given half a chance, I have a feeling you two would make an unbeatable team."

Walters appeared in the doorway and announced that dinner was ready. Rising, L.C. extended his hand to his daughter.

"Is this the same man who endorsed the opposition when the illustrious Mr. Rhodes ran for district attorney?" she murmured, also rising and slipping her arm through his.

"I wasn't sure he was ready for the job. I was wrong. Someday I hope I'll be able to say that to his face and have him believe me."

As they left the study and headed for the dining room, Diana realized it was something she hoped for herself. But the realist in her knew it was a wish that wasn't likely to come true anytime soon.

A week later, Adam was still unable to put the incident with Diana out of his mind. It haunted him. *She* haunted him. It didn't matter if he was alone, or brainstorming with several members of his staff. The mem-

ory of her, like a ghost, would float into his conscious
mind and stun him with the power of a blow to the back
of the head. In a restaurant amid the mouth-watering
scents of chateaubriand and Cabernet Sauvignon, he
would catch a fleeting hint of her perfume and startle
his dinner companion by jerking around in his seat before he even realized who he was looking for. He had
only to see a classical blonde in a crowd and he was
doing double takes. His staff began to inquire about his
health. Muriel began to eye him with increasing dis-
trust.

It was with more relief than professional interest that
he found himself in Houston that Friday, filling in for
a judge as the guest speaker during a luncheon gathering of attorneys. He needed the break, the distance
from Corpus, and it was also why he found himself
phoning Kendall Manning later that afternoon to ask if
she and Braden wouldn't mind some last-minute company.

"What a wonderful surprise," she said an hour later
when he arrived at her front door.

As always, her hug was enthusiastic, her energy a
tangible thing he could feel dancing around her, and it
drew from him one of the few spontaneous smiles he'd
produced in days. He was glad he called. He had few
real friends. She was one of them.

Holding her back by the shoulders, he gave her a
sweeping look, taking in the green sweat suit she wore,
her blond ponytail and the green headband that, like the
suit, matched her sparkling eyes. "You haven't aged a
day since you married that big-lug cop of yours and it's
been what? Two years now?"

"Two and a half, and who're you calling a big lug?"
Braden demanded, emerging from the kitchen with an

armful of baby and a bottle of beer. Taller by inches than Adam's own six feet, and as broad shouldered as a linebacker, he had an undeniable hint of silver in his dark brown hair that framed his craggy face. But if it was true that both men were pushing forty and that it showed more on Braden, his silver eyes also held a contentment that was enviable.

Adam faked a scowl and leaned toward Kendall. "I thought you two told me you'd get rid of this guy so we could be alone?"

"I didn't have the heart." She sighed. "Besides, the thought of having dinner with two handsome hunks was too tempting to resist."

"Three," her husband corrected, handing the lively toddler to Adam. "Here, wise guy, take your godson while I see how the charcoal's doing outside. Matt, old boy, listen up. Uncle Adam is going to tell you all about Brooks Brothers suits, silk ties and why all lawyers have to drive a Mercedes. That should put you to sleep faster than a bedtime story."

"Cute guy, your old man," Adam muttered to the infant, who ignored him because he was already fascinated by the Rolex on Adam's wrist. But the grin he exchanged with the taller man who then turned and headed back toward the kitchen was friendly.

It hadn't always been the case. In the beginning they'd approached each other with suspicion, even dislike, because each in his own way cared for Kendall and was protective of her. It was only after Adam saw for himself that Braden made Kendall happy, and Braden realized Adam's interest in her was based only on friendship and respect, did the two begin to relax around each other.

The arrival of young Matthew twenty-one months ago helped. Adam lifted the child high in his arms until Matt squealed in delight. Except for his dark hair, he was his mother all over again. "But good Lord," he groaned after saying that to Kendall, "he must eat like his father. I think he's twice the size he was at Christmas when you had that picture on my desk made."

"Almost. I think he might end up even bigger than his daddy," she replied, beaming. "Why don't I take him, so you can slip out of your jacket and tie before he tries to stuff those in his mouth, along with your watch?"

"In a second. First we've got to get his present out of the car."

"Oh, Adam," she protested, as he extricated the gold band out of the grip of the child's front teeth. "You can't keep bringing him presents every time you come up here."

"How often do I get up here?"

"Not enough, but you *are* spoiling him."

Adam bounced Matt playfully on his arm. "Tell your mommy it's a godfather's privilege. Hey, bud, guess what Uncle Adam brought you?"

"Car!"

Adam shot Kendall a dry look. "Why do I get the feeling Braden's coaching him? Nice try, pal," he replied to the boy. "Wait until you graduate from Harvard and we'll discuss that. In the meantime, let's go see if second best will do."

Two minutes later, he returned carrying—barely—Matt on top of a giant stuffed elephant. Kendall clasped her hand over her mouth to keep from laughing.

"It's almost as big as his room!"

"Pony!" Matt cried.

"What in blazes—" Braden, coming back into the living room carrying a tray of drinks, simply stared as Adam set toy and child down on the middle of the carpet. "That's just terrific—I can see a slipped lower disk in my future as I carry that and our little bruiser to bed every night. Thanks heaps, Rhodes."

"Anytime, Manning. Anytime."

Braden cooked steaks out on the grill and they ate dinner inside in the dining room while watching Matt play with his new toy, and catching up with what was new in each other's lives.

"I can't believe it's been two and a half years already," Adam murmured, as they lingered over coffee. "Are you still glad you left police work to go into social services?" he asked Kendall.

"Definitely, and now I'm glad you were always lecturing me about doing that."

"Did I lecture?"

"Incessantly, but I forgive you. I also think it's better for our marriage. Braden gets to see some of the kids he's had to arrest start new lives in our programs, and psychologically it's helped him feel that he's making some progress. If we were both still cops, I think that feeling of guilt and helplessness might be stronger."

"Not to mention I don't have to worry myself sick that she's in the middle of a high-speed chase, or a shoot-out," Braden added, rising.

Kendall shook her head. "It's okay for me to worry, but not him."

He reached over, cupped the side of her face and swooped down for a hard, hungry kiss. "I'll always come home to you," he murmured, his voice so deep it was more like a rumble of thunder.

"See that you do," Kendall whispered.

Adam had to look away. The depth of emotion that flared between husband and wife was too poignant even for a friend to share. He'd never in his life experienced a moment like that with a woman. God knows, one never looked at him with such complete adoration. It made him feel empty, and old.

"Come on, tough guy," Braden said, moving to scoop up his son from the floor. "Time to take a bath and hit the sack." He stretched out his arms so that Matt lay belly down across them. "Okay. Show Uncle Adam how you make like a torpedo."

Giggling, Matt slapped his chubby hands over his eyes and began wiggling his sneaker-clad feet. As Braden provided the appropriate sound effects, father and son raced down the hallway.

"I don't know who's the bigger ham," Kendall murmured. But the love shining in her eyes clearly indicated she thought they were wonderful. She caught Adam's bemused look and smiled. "Sorry. Those two have a habit of turning me to mush."

"I'm glad you're happy."

She tilted her head, her look inquiring. "What about you? Are you happy?"

"I guess I'm all right."

"You deserve better than all right."

"I'm afraid there're a few people who would disagree with you."

"Your favorite defense attorney, for instance?"

Adam compressed his mouth into a tighter line. Once he'd made the mistake of mentioning Diana to Kendall. He didn't exactly regret it, but it riled him that even here he couldn't be free of her.

"I think Diana has made it her mission in life to see I'm placed in a padded cell at what's euphemistically called a rest home."

"Oh, dear. I *thought* you seemed a bit more tense than usual. How disappointing.... When I think of her name, I visualize this classy brunette just oozing sophistication."

"Blonde."

"Pardon?"

"You got it all right, but she's a blonde. Pale, like a field of ripe wheat in the moonlight."

"I see." Kendall took another sip of her coffee. "With brown eyes?"

"No, gray. Smoke gray. They make you think of fog, and soft things like rabbits and doves—until she opens her mouth," he added. "Then all I think about is strangling her."

"Her voice irritates you that much?"

"What? No! Her voice is fine. Part of the problem is she uses it too well. I send one of my people to argue a case with her, and within an hour they're as mesmerized as the jury is."

Kendall bit at her lower lip, but her eyes sparkled with laughter. "I had no idea *that* was the problem."

"The problem is she's a sorceress, and you can wipe that grin off your face, because whatever you're thinking, you're wrong."

"Am I?"

"*Yes*, damn it."

"I think you're attracted, Adam."

He gave her his fiercest scowl. "That's all I need."

"Actually, I think it's exactly what you need."

"If I am, I'll get over it, believe me. All I have to do is wait for her to choose her next case."

"Are her legal ethics questionable?"

Adam had to admit that they weren't. "But she's so liberal she's . . . If Jack the Ripper came up for trial today, I'll bet anything she'd find some little something to suggest his innocence so she could justify taking his case."

"I'm sure you're exaggerating."

"Not by much," he grumbled, and reached for his own coffee. "Now can we change the subject, please, before she gives me indigestion in absentia?"

Kendall chuckled and began collecting the dishes on the table. "Okay. Anyway, there was something I wanted to ask you to do for me. Remember the women's shelter I used to beg, borrow and blackmail aid for? Well, they're one of several groups holding a big bazaar tomorrow, and I've been collecting old books for them to sell for weeks, but a mix-up in schedules messed up my plans to get them down there in time."

"And you want me to play Good Samaritan and take them with me tonight," Adam said, feeling dread weigh down his stomach. "You *know* I hate those sorts of things. Let me write them a check. I'll write one for both of us."

"It means more to them when they feel they've earned the money, Adam."

By leaving him alone, he'd happily consider it earned. "May I remind you that I play golf Saturday mornings? I've got a standing reservation for a ten-o'clock tee off. Do you have any idea what some people would do for that slot?"

Kendall nodded patiently. "The bazaar starts at nine. You could drop them off on the way."

"You planned this, didn't you?"

"How could I? I didn't know you were coming until you phoned." She gave him her most entreating look. "Wasn't I always there for you when you needed a body to take to all those parties and fund-raisers?"

"A body?" Wounded, he laid his hand to his chest. "You're making me sound like a Philistine!"

"Didn't I shield you from all those society matrons who were always trying to introduce you to their daughters?"

"All right, all right! I'll do it," he muttered, wishing she was still around to help him out. "But that's all, agreed?"

"Agreed."

"I mean it. If there's something else, some teeny-weeny extra thing you're not telling me about, I'm giving you fair warning somebody's in for a disappointment, because I'm going to drop off the books and leave."

"Fine. Great. Terrific." Kendall held up her hands in surrender before breaking down and giving him an affectionate smile. "I really appreciate this, and I know the ladies of the shelter will, too. I'll even bet that afterward you'll be glad you did it. These sorts of things have a tendency to put your life in a whole new perspective."

Adam's expression remained dour. "I can't wait."

Five

_____

"What do you mean, _no_?"

Beneath the crepe-papered banner designating the Our Lady of Mercy Women's Shelter booth, Adam Rhodes and Muriel Littlejohn stood glaring at each other. People scurried around them, excited with their preparations for the bazaar, which would open in a half an hour. Nails were being hammered, glasses clinked tunefully as boxes were unpacked, and above, the sun promised a glorious spring day. Not exactly the stuff of which nightmares are born, but for Adam it had become one nonetheless.

It was bad enough to have had to bear Muriel's company during the week at the office, but to have her infringing her presence on his days off was asking too much. He didn't even want to know what warped-minded fate thought it would be amusing to torment him like this; he would settle for getting out of there, which was exactly what he was going to do after he impressed a few things upon Muriel.

"I mean exactly what I said," he told her, clasping his hands behind his back and assuming an almost military stance. "No, I will not go crawling around in a dark, dingy basement to locate the rest of your boxes. I agreed to bring *this* box, and I have. Mission accomplished. Obligation fulfilled. Goodbye, Muriel."

"What kind of a man deserts a woman in her hour of need?" she demanded.

"A man who has an appointment in half an hour."

"Appointment," she scoffed as her gaze swept over his dark brown polo shirt and camel-colored slacks. "You're just going to play *golf*."

"How astute! And as far as I recall, it's still not considered a hanging offense."

"Well, the boxes are heavy. How do you expect us to carry them?"

Adam let his own gaze drop over Muriel in her paisley-print tent dress, but judiciously refrained from offering the first piece of advice that came to mind. "I'm sure you'll think of something."

Muriel's eyes filled with reproach. "You're no gentleman, Mr. Rhodes."

"Mr. Rhodes? District Attorney Rhodes?"

Adam turned and found himself face-to-face with a tiny scrub-faced nun who beamed up at him through thick, wire-frame glasses. While a little voice in the back of his head warned of opportunities about to be lost, he cleared his throat and managed a polite smile. "Yes, ma'am. Er, Sister."

"Sister Mary Pauline," she murmured with a dignified bow. "Well, isn't this a joyous day! First we're sent

Muriel to help us tend our booth, and now you. I feel truly blessed.''

"Oh, now wait a minute," Adam began.

"Mr. Rhodes can't stay long, Sister Mary Pauline," Muriel injected quickly. "But he heard we were having problems getting our boxes out of the basement and generously offered to bring them up for us.''

"Wonderful. I was so worried about how we were going to manage that. Our handyman fell off the roof at the home last week and broke his hip, and we've been struggling with preparations as best we can. The girls did a lovely job building the booth, don't you think? But bringing up those boxes . . .''

"Yes, well, you know, Sister—"

"Oh, listen to me prattle," the elderly nun said, shaking her head. "What you need to know is where to find them, don't you? Come with me and I'll show you.''

Adam cast a parting, murderous glance over his shoulder toward Muriel and reluctantly followed. It was one thing to let Muriel think what she may of him, it was entirely another to disappoint a nun. Why, he didn't know—he wasn't even Catholic!

As Sister Mary Pauline led him to the back of the old school building and issued directions, he sighed inwardly. She sounded like she was used to giving a lot of directions. Maybe that handyman didn't fall off the roof; maybe he jumped!

There was nothing to do but to get it over with, he thought, as they came to a halt by the descending stairs. It wasn't as if he didn't actually have time for this, and what were a few boxes and a bit of dust? He could wash up in the men's locker room before he met Judge Perry. Besides, was he really in such a hurry to listen again as

Bernie ran through his itinerary for the cruise he and Emily were about to take?

"Did I confuse you, Mr. Rhodes?"

"Hmm? No, no. Past the boiler room, right turn and the boxes are clearly marked. Got it, Sister."

"I'll get back to the booth, then, and help Muriel set up what we have before the rest of the girls arrive."

Adam's smile held up until she turned away, and as he started down the stairs he shook his head. He *was* a charitable person, he reassured himself. Didn't he send generous checks to a number of needy causes every year? And he worked hard, giving up a lot of his free time to do things that were job oriented but that he didn't get paid for. Why should he be made to feel guilty about wanting to spend his weekends doing what he enjoyed? So what, if only a small percentage of the world's population could afford to relax the way he did? So what if he enjoyed living well? He earned it. Did that make him a snob or an unworthy person?

He blinked and squinted to adjust his vision to the dimness of the storage room. The only light came from a dirt-smeared window, and it was minimal. Still, he could see boxes piled against walls, and in the middle of the room, like miniature pyramids. He stepped aside to let someone carrying one pass, then took a deep breath of musty air and went to find those marked for the shelter.

Twenty minutes later, sweating and covered with an itching layer of dust, he descended the stairs for the last box. Whatever feelings of goodwill he'd talked himself into were gone. The growing smirk on Muriel's face had achieved that. His thoughts were on the shower he knew he now needed. Luckily he kept a change of clothes in his locker at the club, but even so, he was going to cut it close time-wise.

He bent to lift the carton when a voice from above cautioned him.

"Uh-uh... That's mine."

Startled, because he'd believed he was alone, he jerked his head up, his gaze zeroing in on the ladder a few feet away. Up it went along a pair of endless legs, intriguingly covered by a pair of blue slacks, then a matching blue-and-white sweater, to a classically beautiful but all-too-familiar face. "Oh, hell," he muttered. "You're all I need."

Recovering from her own surprise, Diana produced a smile that was quick and sardonic. "Nice to see you, too." She turned to rest one arm across the top of the stepladder and placed her right hand on her trim hip. "What brings the Honorable Adam Barclay Rhodes to such a plebeian gathering? I thought this was your day to race your motorized chariot across the fairways at Westbrook?"

Adam straightened, too tired to feel anything but resignation. "Tell me," he asked, drawing his forearm across his gritty and damp brow. "Does that mouth of yours ever run down?"

Diana drew her lower lip between her teeth, stung by his response when she'd been expecting something completely different. He was right; she was on remote control with him. When was she going to learn to wait before going on the offensive the moment they came face-to-face? What right did she have to mock him? He was here, wasn't he? Working and undeniably tired.

"That was rude of me," she murmured. "I think it's good of you to be here helping out."

Uncomfortable with the knowledge that he was only here out of duress, he quickly changed the subject. "What group are you with?"

"All of them, I guess. I'm cochairing the bazaar. You?"

"The women's shelter." Embarrassed at the way that sounded, he laughed, then shrugged.

"No, I think that's great."

"Yeah, well, Muriel's helping, too." God, he prayed, please don't let them run into each other or I'll never live this down. What was wrong with him? He was actually trying to *impress* her. But she did look more approachable this way, what with her hair falling free around her shoulders and all. Softer. He swallowed, aware of how dry his throat had become. "I was just getting this last box because I really do have to leave."

"But it's not your box. Check out the other label on the side. See? I think you've got all of yours. That one goes with this one I was trying to—"

"Look out!"

She realized that the cardboard was old and disintegrating the moment she gave it a tug. A large piece came off in her hand, and the force of her pull caused her to lose her balance, sending both her and the ladder toppling.

Adam managed to push the ladder into the opposite direction while grabbing her around the waist with his other arm. But it sent them spinning sideways, and they tumbled into the pile of dusty sheets that had been used to cover everything.

It wasn't necessary to ask her if she was all right; she began laughing before he had a chance to catch his breath and determine his own condition. Yet he wasn't annoyed, either. The caressing sweep of her hair and the arousing movements of her body as she shifted against him dried up his own reservoir of sarcasm, leaving only the memory of the last time she'd been this close.

"Lucky for you I don't weigh more," she said, trying to raise herself on her elbows.

"Oh, I don't know. The androgynous look can be hazardous. There's nothing quite like being impaled by a sharp hip to keep a man's reflexes in order."

"Andro—I am not! I have enough of everything."

He let his gaze drop to her breasts. "Almost."

Indignant, she began to climb off him, but just as quickly he pulled her back down, then rolled over until she was beneath him.

"Now who can't take a joke?"

"Was *that* a joke?"

Her haughty tone made him smile, the feel of her body beneath him made him realize again how well they suited each other. His gaze shifted to her hair, fanning out in pale splendor. "It's been a long time since I've seen it loose," he murmured, extending his fingers to touch.

Diana's heartbeat accelerated a notch. "It's probably a mess. I should have tied it back."

"No, I—" He caught himself just in time. Yes, he liked it loose, he liked seeing his hands buried in it, and he wanted more than this moment of feeling himself pressing into her softness. He wanted to be buried there, watch her go wild beneath him, lose himself in her. But how could he? There was so much more than cloth separating them. "Diana," he began, his voice gruff, restrained.

"Just do it," she whispered, slipping her arms around his neck to pull herself up toward him. "Kiss me."

The hell with it, he thought, fastening his mouth to hers. What did any of it matter, compared to this gut-wrenching need to touch and taste? He pressed her back onto the sheets, let her draw him closer yet, and gave himself up to the pleasure of simply feeling.

She kissed as no woman he'd ever kissed did—without hesitation or feigned coyness. With the honest sensuality he'd only begun to appreciate last time, she met the demanding thrust of his tongue and matched his rhythmic strokes in a silent dance as old as time. A caldron of heat deep in his belly boiled over and spread to his tensed loins. He pressed closer, but the heat only grew worse; still he didn't, couldn't stop and soon the musky scented sheets whispered like a twilight breeze beneath the feverish movements of their bodies.

As he tore his mouth from hers to run his lips down her throat, Diana arched her neck to give him better access. She raked her fingers deep into his hair, massaging the corded muscles at his nape. *Yes*, she wanted to tell him. *More. Harder.* But she didn't dare, because she didn't want to take the chance of destroying the moment.

Yet, inside, her heart swelled with emotion. This was as it was meant to be between them. Let him fight her about anything else if he must, but here there could be no arguments; here they were alike. They belonged together.

She didn't feel him undo the tiny pearl buttons on the front of her sweater. Such nimble fingers. She wanted to laugh as the excitement went straight to her head in a rush like champagne. When he traced his thumbs over the provocative but useless lace of her bra and brought his mouth down to follow, the only sound she made was that of her breath shuddering as it came in and went out.

She wanted to feel him, too, and pulled his shirt free from his slacks. She'd seen him as a younger man at the country club, dressed in little more than swim trunks, and knew that he was lean; not obviously muscled, but strong. She wanted to run her hands over the contours of the mature man, splay her fingers through the golden hair on his chest, watch his tautly muscled abdomen grow rock hard when she ran her lips over it.

But as he began to slide the straps of her bra down her arms, there was a crash outside and she grabbed his wrists.

"Adam, we *can't*—not here."

He wasn't sure what got to him first, the sudden tension in her body or the panic in her voice, but he, too, went still, and a moment later—after realizing what she'd said—he swore under his breath. *Had he lost his mind?*

He rolled away from her and Diana sat up, quickly rebuttoning her sweater. "I heard something fall outside and realized where we were." She stood up and combed her fingers through her hair. "I wasn't playing a game," she added softly.

He believed her, but he still couldn't bring himself to turn around and face her. It wasn't only who she was; it was what she had accomplished. He'd almost lost his head with her. Another moment or two and... The prospect shook him. He wasn't some randy teenager, yet she had reduced him to having the needs of one.

"I have to go," he muttered.

Diana stopped brushing dust off her clothing, an unpleasant feeling beginning to crawl over her. "Yes, of course. You said there was someplace you needed to be." She swallowed her pride and added, "Can we meet later—just to talk?"

"I don't think that would be a good idea." He took a few steps, called himself a fool and swung back around. It was a mistake. Her gray eyes were shimmering pools full of disbelief and hurt. "Look, it was a mistake. I take full responsibility."

Her chin lifted, pride returning. "I see," she whispered. "We're still on that same old song and dance. Anyone but me would have been fine, is that it?"

"Diana—"

"Get out."

"I'm thinking about what's best for both of us."

Her laugh was bitter and not quite steady. "Oh, spare me that. You're thinking of yourself. Justin should see you now—he'd be proud to know you turned into a chip off the old block."

Adam drew a deep breath, but held his temper. "All right, maybe you think I deserved that. I suppose that makes us even."

"What that makes us is fools; me for believing you could change, and you for not seeing what's right in front of your nose. Now go away and let me get back to work."

He did, only because he didn't know what else to say. If he looked back, he might have thought of something. Diana straightened the ladder, sat down on the bottom rung and buried her face in her hands.

She didn't drink or smoke, and her attitude toward sports and most forms of exercise these days was one of ambivalence, so when it became evident that she needed to get her mind off her problems, Diana could only think of two options—work or become interested in someone else. She chose work.

April blossomed into May, daffodils gave way to irises and roses. In the office, secretaries and clerks paraded their latest spring fashions and the chief topic of conversation in the break room was who was going where during vacation. Diana barely noticed. It became painfully obvious one morning when she stopped to refill her coffee cup on her way back from the reference library.

Andy was by the refrigerator with another secretary, pouring herself a cup of healthful vegetable juice. The two younger women were in the midst of a lively conversation until Andy interrupted it to turn to Diana.

"What do you think I should do, pack more evening wear or casual stuff?"

Diana frowned at the way the dark brew looked, before glancing up at her. "Excuse me? Pack for what?"

Andy rolled her expressive eyes. "My vacation. The cruise I'm taking in ten days, remember? Where is your mind lately?"

"On business," Diana snapped back. "Which is where yours should be, considering that's what we pay you for."

The room grew as quiet as a mausoleum. Aware of everyone's eyes on her, Diana felt her hand shake as she replaced the coffeepot. It was a relief to get out of there, but all the way down the hallway her cheeks burned with embarrassment. How could she have been such a witch—and to Andy, no less, who never once complained when asked to stay late to type a brief or a piece of correspondence that simply had to make the evening mail. It made Diana feel lower than a worm, and she felt even worse when she discovered Oscar waiting for her back in her office.

"I hope this isn't going to take long," she told him, not bothering to try to hide her weariness. "I have to be in court in two hours and there's a mountain of things I need to take care of before I leave."

She sat down behind her desk and tried not to bristle when he unfolded the morning edition of the newspaper and dropped it in front of her.

"*This* is the Porter case you mentioned taking in yesterday's meeting? *This* is how I have to learn that the woman's a cold-blooded murderess?"

Diana ignored the paper because she'd seen it herself hours earlier, and took a sip of her bitterly strong coffee. "All she needs is sentencing, eh, Oscar?"

"That's a captious argument, and you know it."

Oscar, pacing, brushed back his somber black suit jacket and slipped his hands into his pants pockets. It was a familiar gesture usually signaling that a lecture was inevitable, and Diana glanced down at her watch, wondering what else was going to go wrong today.

"The woman *admitted* emptying that revolver into her husband," he began. "Her fingerprints on the weapon concur with her confession to the police. Pray tell me what jury will need to hear more for a conviction?"

"Oscar, I warned you that it was going to be a case of self-defense. Alice Porter is a victim of wife abuse; her hospital records read like a horror story; before the police could book her, she had to be taken to the emergency room to have her hand X-rayed and her eye stitched."

"You honestly believe you can get her off with that excuse?"

"It's not an excuse. If Alice hadn't stopped Carl Porter, he would have killed her."

"Do you realize what kind of reflection a case like this can have on the firm? On your reputation if you lose?"

"Then I'd better not lose, had I?"

He shot her a stern look. "What does L.C. have to say about this?"

"I wouldn't know; I haven't asked him."

"Haven't..." He reached into an inside pocket in his jacket and pulled out a handkerchief, then proceeded to dab it against his brow. "Oh, dear. It doesn't feel good. It doesn't feel good at all."

Having heard more than enough, Diana put away her coffee and refolded the paper. "I'm sorry if you're unhappy with the case," she told him, handing it back to him. "But my position stands. And now, if there's nothing else, I really do have a tight schedule."

"You'll keep me abreast of things?" he asked, hesitating at the door.

Diana's answering smile was grim. "Your confidence in me is inspiring, Oscar. On your way out, would you tell Andrea that I'd like to see her, please?"

She slipped on her glasses and reached for one of the files in front of her. Check with L.C. indeed, she thought, gritting her teeth together. As a full partner, her decision to take a case or not was her own. Granted, the associates held a daily meeting to discuss new clients and pending cases, but it was—for the most part—a formality. She hadn't needed to "get permission" to take a case since her first job after graduation from law school, and she wasn't about to start now. She *definitely* didn't need this aggravation.

After beginning to read the writ before her for the third time, Diana removed her glasses and massaged the bridge of her nose. No doubt about it, she was going to have to start delegating more of her caseload to one of the newer associates if she intended to get any meaningful work done.

"Did you need something?"

Hearing the coolness in Andy's voice, Diana grimaced inwardly. Did she ever, beginning with a chance to take back the last ten minutes. She waved her inside and closed the file. Why was it that the people you cared for the most were the ones you ended up hurting? she wondered.

"Sit down for a minute. An apology is in order."

Andy's expression warmed considerably. "You don't have time."

"I'll make some." She gave her an aggrieved look. "Andy, I'm sick over what I said to you. Forgive me?"

"I know you didn't mean it."

"That's no excuse."

"You're busier than ever."

"Agreed, but—"

"And there's Mr. Fontaine to worry about."

Once again Diana counted her blessings for the day this young woman walked into her office. She was one of the few people besides Oscar and Martin who she herself had confided with about L.C.'s condition, and her trustworthiness alone made her a treasure. "You're supposed to make me grovel a bit," she murmured drolly.

Andy dismissed that with a shake of her head. "I'm worried about you. I thought Mr. Fontaine was doing better."

"The tests show that he is."

"Then there's something else. Something besides too much work, which you normally flourish under."

Vanity had never been one of Diana's vices, but she couldn't help asking. "Does it show?"

"To someone who knows you, it does. Oh, the outer shell is still terrific, but I have a feeling you just put yourself on automatic pilot when you get up these days, and don't think twice about what you're doing or what you put on. I mean, how bad is a person going to look in a Saint Laurent suit, right?"

"Thanks—I think."

"But when was the last time you looked outside and noticed the world is passing you by?"

"I knew there had to be a flip side to this."

"Diana, it's spring! People are getting tans, wearing white, drinking Chablis al fresco. You look like you're expecting another 'Texas blue norther' to come plowing through any minute."

She glanced down at her charcoal-gray suit and had to admit it was almost as somber looking as Oscar's. Had she allowed Adam to get to her this deeply?

She gave her secretary a rueful smile. "Okay, I hear you."

"Yeah, but will you do anything about it?"

Trying to lighten the mood, Diana placed one hand over her heart and made a Girl Scout salute with the other. "I will definitely not take my bad mood out on you, and strive to dress in a more seasonable fashion."

Andy tilted her head and gave her a speculative look. "What you really need is to have an affair."

"Consider two out of three the best ratio you're going to get, my friend. Right now, men aren't among my most favorite species."

"Aha! I knew it." The younger woman gave her a quirky smile. "Well, you know what they say. There's nothing like a man to make you forget a man."

But she didn't *want* to forget Adam. Strangle him, maybe. Have a blazing affair with him, definitely. Fall in love and dream dreams with him. . . .

"Yoo-hoo . . . Earth to boss lady. Where'd you just go?"

Diana's answering smile was grim. "To a hanging."

"I asked if you were going to the fund-raiser tonight—the one for the new music hall." Andy tapped her pencil, indicating the notation on Diana's desk calendar.

"Blast . . . That's tonight?" Diana was hardly in the mood to attend, but she'd already missed another event and turned down two dinner invitations in the past few weeks.

"Martin already phoned once to ask if you wanted a ride."

"No, you'd better call him back and tell him I'll take my own car. I'm not sure when I'll get out of court, and I've got errands to run afterward. Tell him I'll see him there."

"Promise me you'll wear something sleek and sexy?"

"Oh, get out of here so I can get back to work," Diana groaned, but her eyes lit with amusement. When Andy was almost at the door, she called out to her. "About that question you asked earlier? Just bring extra money. You can always buy what you need during a stop in port. And, Andy? Thanks."

When Diana finally did make it to the downtown hotel that night, she was forty minutes late and the ballroom was packed. At least it made it less noticeable that she'd arrived unescorted, she thought, negotiating her way through the crowd.

"Diana, darling—"

Diana dug her short nails into her beaded evening bag, but forced herself to smile cordially as she turned to Margo Reed, wife of a wealthy oilman and chairwoman of this event. "Hello, Margo," she replied, not quite able to match the statuesque brunette's enthusiasm. "You've done a splendid job, as always."

"One tries. You look stunning—though blue is a blonde's color, isn't it?"

Actually the shimmering V-neck gown was aqua, but Diana didn't bother correcting her because she knew what Margo really wanted was a compliment in kind. Unfortunately the emerald-green taffeta creation, with all its ruffles, made the older woman look like a float in the Cotton Bowl parade.

"Well, no one holds a candle to you tonight," she murmured.

Pleased, Margo drew her toward her circle of companions. "Come say hello."

Diana felt the smile on her lips freeze the moment her eyes locked with Adam's. So much for wondering if he would be here, she thought, and for hoping she could avoid him. One by one she greeted the others while, inside, her heart began to thud crazily, like a jackhammer gone out of control.

Finally she had no choice but to meet his direct stare. "Good evening, Adam." Thank goodness. At least her voice remained in control.

"Diana."

He looked no more pleased to see her than she him, but he did look devastating, as usual, in his formal wear. Did anyone else feel the air crackle between them?

she wondered. It seemed impossible that they could miss it, yet she hoped they would simply consider it an extension of their usual animosity toward each other.

"Is L.C. coming tonight?" the mayor asked. "We rarely get to see him these days."

"He's preoccupied with a new project," she replied easily enough, because it was the truth. "He's writing his memoirs."

"No? Good for him!"

"The old fox better leave me out of it," someone else grumbled.

"I, for one, expect an honorable mention," Margo drawled, earning a chuckle from the others. It was no secret that once she and L.C. had been rumored to be an item, until she'd eloped with her oilman.

"We noticed you made the front page of the paper today," said a developer Diana barely knew.

She tried to play it down by shrugging. "It's not a low-profile story." The last thing she wanted to do was talk about the article, with Adam standing three feet away.

"Adam just told us he's decided to try the case himself. Looks like you two are *really* going to get to butt heads this time."

Unable to cover her surprise, Diana's gaze swung back to Adam, only to find him still watching her. His expression was enigmatic, but she knew now that the tension she sensed in him wasn't only for what had happened between them two weeks ago. He, too, was angry she'd taken Alice Porter's case, and by facing her in court he was publicly proving his displeasure.

"Well," she murmured, collecting herself. "Butting heads is certainly what we do best, isn't it, Adam?"

"Unfortunately."

Was that a flicker of regret she saw in his eyes? Before she had a chance to analyze it, someone stepped behind her and lightly grasped her by the shoulders. She glanced back and saw it was Martin.

"Hello, everyone." He shifted his hold to lace his fingers through Diana's. "Excuse us, won't you? They're playing our song."

Diana went along with the lie, but as soon as they were on the dance floor and he turned her into his arms, she gave him a skeptical look. "This doesn't sound like the alma mater from Yale University to me."

"Give me a break. I got you away from there before Count Dracula could sharpen his teeth on you, didn't I?" He leaned back, his sweeping gaze assessing. "And from the looks of things, I was just in time. Nice dress, but you've been through a wringer or two since I last saw you."

"Compliments were never your strong point, dear."

"I said I liked the dress."

"Alas, there's a hag in it."

He couldn't quite contain his laughter. "Poor Di. Does your ego need stroking?" He lowered his mouth to her ear. "What I meant to say is that you're looking fragile tonight, rather like a Monet water lily on a quicksilver pool."

Diana felt her eyes fill with unexpected tears. She tried to duck her head, but she wasn't quick enough and Martin saw them. His teasing smile turned into a frown and he tucked her closer into his arms.

"Okay, tell Uncle Marty what's wrong. Did our mercurial district attorney take a too-deep bite out of you? Want me to challenge him to a duel? We can meet at Westbrook at dawn...his choice of woods...may the best swing win. I'll aim for his aristocratic nose and yell *Viva la Fontaine!* before he knocks my lights out.''

''Will you stop before I start bawling and embarrass both of us.''

Martin sighed and brushed his lips across her temple. ''He *did* say something rotten, didn't he?''

''No, not really. I guess I'm just tired.''

''Uh-huh. Well, I was wondering when it was going to catch up with you,'' he grumbled. ''Do you know you walked right past me in the courthouse lobby last Wednesday. Never saw me.''

She uttered a sound of disgust. ''I've been doing a lot of that lately.''

''Ignoring friends?''

''Or insulting them. Take your pick.''

Martin was silent a moment. ''I heard Adam's going to prosecute in the Porter case.''

''It was bound to happen sooner or later.''

''Considering what you already have on your plate, later might have been more fair. Anyway, I just want you to know that I'm here for you. If you ever need to talk, you've only to pick up the phone and call me.''

Diana lifted her head to plant a tender kiss on his cheek. ''I think I'd rather hear about what's new with you right now. How's Lisa?''

''Resisting me.''

''Crazy woman.''

''Lucky for her I'm tenacious.''

''The second-most important quality a woman looks for in a man.''

They began to joke about what was the first, and slowly the tension began to ease out of Diana. One song drifted into another. Neither of them saw Adam approaching, until he touched Martin's shoulder.

"May I?"

"If we say no, will you go away?" Diana heard the sting in her voice and felt Martin's surprised response, but she couldn't help herself. The wound his rejection caused still throbbed.

Rather than answer, Adam deftly drew her out of Martin's arms and into his own. "You might say no, but Prescott's too much of a gentleman to abandon good manners, aren't you, Prescott?"

"I'm considering turning over a new leaf."

Adam cocked an eyebrow, though he told himself he shouldn't be surprised, considering the way Diana looked tonight. What man wouldn't want to keep her to himself?

"How about holding off any radical displays of chivalry for the next five minutes?" he murmured, dropping the menace from his own voice. "I assure you I'm in no mood to poach."

"And I assure *you* that I'm not worried," Martin drawled. With a parting wink to Diana, he left them.

"I'm impressed," Adam said, leading her in the opposite direction around the dance floor. "Obviously you inspire strength as well as passion in your men."

Diana kept her gaze pinned to his bow tie, but inside she was seething.

"Are you lovers, Diana?"

"I don't see that it's any of your business—*you're hurting my hand!*"

"Be glad it's not your neck. Answer me."

"Martin is a *friend*," she whispered angrily, glaring at him. "And what do you care anyway?"

If only he had an answer to that. It was a question he'd been asking himself over and over, and now with her confession warming him like a balm, relief was an-

other emotion that needed explaining. He resisted it—
and the urge to draw her closer—reminding himself it
wasn't the reason he'd come to her.

"Why did you go to the press with the news you were
taking the Porter case?" he asked her. "Are you hoping that the publicity will force a change of venue, and
that by moving the trial to a different city you'll be able
to find a more sympathetic jury?"

"Is that what you think?" She paused to swallow,
trying to remove the slight tremor from her voice. "I
don't know how the press got hold of the story, but it
wasn't through me or my office. I want Alice tried here.
Once this is over, she has to live here; she can't afford
to pack up and move somewhere and start all over
again. She needs to show these people that she was as
much of a victim as anyone was; that she had no choice
but to defend herself."

"Any cop will tell you that one bullet is self-defense,
maybe even two. But six is murder."

"I don't expect you to agree or even understand," she
murmured, glancing away.

His laugh was abrupt and hard. "'Understand'?
You're right there."

"Adam." Her voice was a strangled whisper. In
her eyes were shadows of a soul-deep weariness.
"Please...can't we just be nice to each other for a moment?"

Because she was right, because he'd been unable to
think of little else than what it was like to hold her for
weeks now, fury got tangled with all the other emotions locked inside him and when he drew her closer, his
touch, as well as his voice, was rougher than he meant
them to be.

"Damn it, Diana."

She almost laughed, but it would have come out a sob. "Very romantic."

His chest rose and fell with a deep breath. "I don't want this."

"Neither do I."

But neither of them moved to leave, and for the next hundred heartbeats or so there was only the music and the dance. Was it by osmosis that they agreed that words, for the moment, were too much of a gamble? Who first relaxed against whom?

Unable to resist it, Adam slid both arms around her and lowered his head so that his cheek rested against the smooth silk of her hair. Diana wrapped her arms around his neck and stroked her fingers against the warm skin at his nape. Yet they couldn't quite forget that there were others around who would watch and speculate.

"You left your hair loose again."

"I was running late and only had time to blow-dry it."

"I thought it a deliberate attempt to torment me. I should have told you how lovely you look tonight. Instead, I was rude."

"Tell me now," she whispered, feeling a recklessness that was as dangerous as it was exciting.

The fingers at her waist tightened, drawing her closer, so there was no mistaking that he felt everything she did. "I want you," he breathed. "Heaven help me, but I do."

"No one's ever prayed for divine intervention to save themselves from me."

"Then you didn't want them and they didn't feel the full strength of your power, did they?" His pale eyes lasered into hers. "Diana?"

"No."

He slid his other hand up beneath the heavy fall of her hair and caressed her nape, coaxing her to rest her head against his shoulder. He couldn't risk looking into her eyes again. Whatever this was between them, it was racing madly toward a boiling point, and this was neither the time nor the place. As it was, he was hard-pressed not to slide his hands down her silk-clad hips.

"This can't go on," he rasped.

"I know it."

"You were right. We need to talk."

"But not now," Martin murmured, suddenly reappearing beside them.

Diana saw the questions in his eyes, as well as some shrewd analysis, but the grim set to his mouth made her sense there was something else on his mind. "What is it?" she demanded urgently.

"It's Rose. Leon was arrested again, this time for stealing a car. When Rose went down to the police station she collapsed. It's a heart attack, Diana."

"Oh, no."

"She's been taken to the hospital. I'll drive you there."

"I can do that," Adam told him. He looked back at Diana, not liking her sudden paleness or the haunted quality that had returned to her eyes. Suddenly he saw it all—the stress and the vulnerability. She didn't look as if she could take a lot more.

"Thank you both," she murmured, pulling herself together and giving them each a reassuring smile. "But I've got my own car and it's undoubtedly going to be a long night."

"I could go to the station and see about Leon," Martin offered.

She shook her head. "He's not like you remember him. I'd better handle it. I'll call," she assured him. Then she turned to Adam. *What do I say to you?* her gaze asked.

"Drive carefully," he murmured. "I'll be in touch."

"Fair enough."

Adam watched until she disappeared into the lobby of the hotel, and felt an emptiness that left him chilled. Turning to Martin, he found him watching him with a mixture of astonishment and suspicion.

"Can I buy you a drink?" he asked Adam.

When they'd got Adam's Scotch and Martin's bourbon, they found a quiet corner, but it was Adam who started with the questions.

"Obviously this Rose is important to Diana, but who is she?"

Martin gave him a brief history of Rose Warren's relationship to the Fontaine family. "So they're close," he concluded. "And I'm worried because this could be the last straw for Diana. She's got too much to deal with right now, and if she should lose Rose, what with the threat of—oh, damn."

Adam frowned. "Don't shut down now. Go ahead and finish it. I need to know."

"Why?" Martin was first and foremost Diana's friend. "I know what I think I saw out there on that dance floor, and it explains a lot of the tension between you two. But what does it mean?"

"I don't know, and even if I did, I wouldn't discuss it with anyone but Diana," Adam replied, meeting Martin's hard look with a harder one.

Martin took a long sip of his drink and thought it over. "She'll have my head if you abuse this information. Worse, it'll break her."

"I think the one thing I can promise you is that I don't want to hurt her."

"I hope not." Martin sighed. "It's L.C. He's got cancer. They're treating it, but you know how that goes."

And in all the months since she'd been back, Adam thought, he'd accused her of plotting against him, taken her appeals to let bygones be bygones and flung them all back in her face.

Martin took another sip of his drink. "Yup, you've been a real sweetheart," he drawled.

As Adam set down his glass on a side table, he barely heard him. He only knew he needed to think, and to do that he wanted a clearer head. And solitude.

It was hours before he wondered if he remembered to say anything to Martin, or had he simply walked out? Considering everything else that weighed on his mind, he decided it hardly mattered.

Six

Fog blanketed the earth and muffled sound like a mother encouraging a child to sleep. Dawn was near—mauve and tangerine tints were already blending together in the eastern sky. As a child Diana loved mornings like this, particularly if there was no school and she could burrow deeper into her comfortable bed to await the songs of birds and the waking of the breeze. Innocent days—and gone. Even if she did crawl into bed now, she rationalized, she knew she was overtired and too wound-up to sleep.

Instead she walked along the beach, grateful for the time, and the fog that kept others inside, affording her some privacy from neighbors who might wonder at her risking the ruination of a seven-hundred-dollar dress with salt water. The damp air held a chill and she walked with her arms wrapped around herself, but the stance was more psychologically than physically motivated: she barely felt the coolness; she *did* feel desolate.

Rose was in critical condition in the ICU and Leon was spending his first night in jail. Neither was out of the woods yet, and Diana was feeling partially responsible. It had been her decision to leave Leon in jail overnight. Even if she could have arranged for bail, after seeing Rose in intensive care, worn-out and hooked up to all those machines, Diana's fury with Leon had grown and she'd assured his sisters he was in the best place for the time being.

She was still angry, and she knew she needed to get past that before she went back to see him later today. Decisions needed to be made, and some of her options didn't sit well with her at all.

She drew a deep breath only to sneeze. "Right, Fontaine," she muttered, sniffing inelegantly. "Catch pneumonia. That'll *really* solve all your problems."

She turned back to the house, wondering if she'd remembered to set her coffee maker last night and if a pot of steaming brew would be ready when she got back. Maybe after a few cups of coffee and a hot soak in the tub she could clear her head enough to think. There might even be time to dwell on last night and Adam. Those few minutes with him had been so special. But she was probably just kidding herself, she thought, a sad smile touching her lips. Even if he *had* experienced a change of heart, nothing could come of it; who would want a woman who didn't even have time for an affair?

As she stepped farther away from the foaming surf, her dejected sigh was covered by the first breeze of the morning.

* * *

He'd never been to her house before. He hadn't even known the address until he called and woke Prescott up a half hour ago to ask him for it. Discovering she lived on the beach—a place he must have driven by countless times over the past months—left him with a strange feeling. As he circled the salmon-pink and white stone house and ducked under a vine-covered trellis that led to the back, it intensified.

She hadn't answered the door and it was doing dangerous things to his resolve. Logic dictated that since she was home she should be asleep, dead to the world; but he wasn't feeling very logical, and all his rationalizing was negative, summing up to the deduction that she didn't want to see him. Unfortunately, after driving around all night he'd come to only one conclusion: *he* needed to see *her*. Could a man say that to a woman without getting a door slammed in his face? Was it enough?

As he walked, he was aware of the lush landscaping, but only because it closed in on him like a jungle. Vines crept up and over the privacy fence, palms and banana trees stood tall, the fog giving them the illusion of being half plant and half beast. Impatient with the fanciful thought, he brushed a wide branch out of his way and rounded the corner to the back deck.

It was painted white like the trim and half covered with a lattice roof. There were more plants in giant clay pots and rattan furniture, but he barely gave it all more than a cursory glance, because his gaze fell and stayed on the evening sandals and purse lying on the third step.

So it wasn't over yet. She wasn't answering the door because she wasn't inside. But where was she? Appeasement was quickly replaced with frustration. She'd picked a helluva time for a stroll.

He swung around—in time to see her emerge from the fog, a Nereid, lifting her gown from the sand with one hand and brushing her hair back from her face with the other. His annoyance raced out of his body along with his breath. He still couldn't explain all the reasons why he had come, but suddenly he knew he wouldn't allow her to send him away.

Diana didn't look up until she was almost upon him, and then it was only because she had a strange feeling. When she saw him, she froze, telling herself it couldn't be, even as she prayed it was. *You're losing your mind,* she warned herself, either that or she was delirious from fever. He wouldn't do this, not Adam. Yet those were his eyes piercing into her with the intensity of a pale blue laser, causing her pulse to turn erratic and her body to feel flushed.

When he extended his hand, she never thought to ignore it. It was her fantasy; she would be a fool not to accept it.

He was still dressed in his black tuxedo, though his bow tie was gone, and the top buttons of his pleated shirt were open. His hair looked like he'd raked his hands through it more than once; a night's growth of beard marked his jaw. Had he been up all night, as well? she wondered, staring into his slightly bloodshot eyes. Why? Where? The questions raced like her heartbeat, but they remained unspoken.

She was trembling. He felt it in her fingertips and from thigh to breast he drew her against him. Fatigue or nerves? He framed her face with his other hand, using his thumb at her jaw to tilt it back so he could study her more closely.

Whatever makeup she'd worn last night was gone, subduing her beauty but not detracting from it. It was her eyes that held his answer; the sadness and exhaustion caused a wrenching inside him he found disturbing. But it was their yearning that made him stiffen against the shudder rising from deep within.

"Say something," she whispered.

Instead he kissed her—not gently as he should have, but with all those warring, pent-up emotions that were tearing him apart. Insistent, he locked his mouth on hers before sliding his tongue deeply to take, and to ask.

He felt her grab hold of the satin-trimmed jacket lapels. Was it to push him away or to get closer? Just in case he framed her face with both hands, imprisoning her, compelling her to accept that this time there would be no backing away for either of them.

Diana wasn't about to back away, but she knew a moment of panic, an instant of needing to recover her balance. A fury desired and released was a fury still; all blind energy with no certain path, no guarantees. Her choice was instinctive; she'd made it even before he reached out to her, and her mind welcomed the whirlwind of madness she knew they could explore together, the momentary oblivion she needed. Despite that acceptance, her heart cried for an assurance that in the end it would mean more than passion and release. When he slid his mouth down the tender column of her throat, her heart forfeited dreams to desperation.

Her soft moan, the subtle surrender he sensed as she relaxed against him, stirred him more than a caress, and he shifted his hold to mold and claim. How achingly slender she was. He sought all her curves and hollows, only to be tormented further by the reminder of how insignificant two layers of silk were in a man's hands.

Through it her heat poured, searing him. He knew it would only be a moment more before the remainder of his restraint had burned away.

"Inside," he muttered, already drawing her to the stairs.

She followed in a daze, bemused; watched him pick up her things. Her sandals looked fragile, erotic in his masculine hands.

He took the key she retrieved from her purse and unlocked the back door. Still silent. It made her pounding heart feel like a kettledrum thumping in her chest.

Once inside, he tossed her things onto a nearby chair and locked the door behind them. Diana stood in the middle of the living room waiting, strangely excited. Wasn't he going to say anything?

"Adam."

He crossed over to her and kissed her again, a hot, arousing kiss that left her clinging weakly to him. She was barely aware of him glancing around, but when he lifted her into his arms and strode down the hallway with her, she couldn't resist the faintest of smiles.

"Which one?" he asked, pausing between four doors.

Unable to tear her gaze away from his face, she indicated the door on the left. He would have made a splendid Viking, she decided, stroking the beginnings of his golden beard, all arrogance and fierce determination. Nothing would stand in his way—she traced her finger over his lower lip only to have it captured between his teeth a second later—nothing, not even an independent and equally determined woman.

She didn't realize he'd passed through the master bedroom and had carried her into the bathroom until she heard the rush of water from the shower as he turned on the taps full blast. A moment later, she realized his intention to step inside with them still fully clothed.

"No!" She blocked the opening with her extended arm. "Are you mad? We're not exactly dressed in wash and wear."

"Have you noticed you're trembling from the cold?" he demanded, his voice gruff. "I won't have you getting ill because of me."

Trembling? So she was. But she quickly dismissed it to focus on what else he said. Her eyes grew soft and teasing. "'I won't have...' Did anyone ever tell you you're a born dictator, Adam?"

"Never mind," he grumbled, setting her on her feet, only to begin stripping them both out of their clothes. "Just don't you start."

The dark threat in his voice caused a delicious shiver that had nothing to do with cold to race down her spine. "Or else what?" she whispered, as her gown pooled around her feet.

Damn her for a witch, he thought, his gaze raking over her sylphlike body, covered only by a teddy the color of her gown. Was she intent on taking what little sanity he had left? He snaked an arm around her waist, dragged her against him and crushed his mouth to hers; and it was in that volcanic temper he carried her beneath the steaming water, not caring a whit if he was still wearing most of his own clothes.

Diana gasped, her senses under assault: water blinding her, his body pinning her to the tiled wall and his mouth inflicting its own sensual torture on hers. But this was what she wanted—at least this first time—she thought, raking her fingers into his hair to draw him closer. She wanted the storm, the demands, the primordial hunger. Let them understand each other this way, first.

His shirt stuck to him like a jealous mistress. Impatient to get to the taut muscles beneath it, she tugged, sending a button, then his cuff links, flying. His laugh was low, and he showed her how much easier she was to undress, peeling away satin, then tasting her as he would a piece of succulent fruit.

But exploration was a fleeting indulgence, accelerated by their mutual urgency. When they were both naked, Adam lifted Diana into his arms and pressed her back against the tiles, intent to have it done.

"Look at me," he demanded, filling her.

Their eyes met and their bodies shuddered. They could see how close they were to the crest; could feel it.

A tiny aching sound broke from her lips. "Hurry," she whispered into his mouth.

He groaned her name in protest, but took what he knew now was his. Was it right or wrong, or did any of that matter at a time like this? As a sweet savage joy pulsed, then exploded between them, he gave up wondering, blotting out everything but the knowledge that in this, at least, they were one.

When the fog that clouded his brain had cleared, Adam gently eased Diana downward until she could stand on her own two feet. But he encouraged her to continue to hold on to him as he held her, running his hands over her supple curves with lazy fascination.

"We're running out of hot water," he murmured, touching his lips to her temple.

"Not to mention causing a flood." Diana glanced down at the water rising around their ankles and their clothes blocking the drain, before giving him an impish smile. "It looks like you're my prisoner for a while. How do you look in a towel?"

"Irresistible." He shut off the water, stepped out of the cubicle and pulled an emerald-green bath sheet off the towel rack. "Come here and I'll show you."

He looked like a god standing there, bronzed from the sun. When he flung the towel around his shoulders and held the ends out for her to join him, she went to him as eagerly as before and pressed her lips to his heart. *Don't let him be sorry,* she prayed.

Adam wrapped her close and lowered his head to hers. Tenderness mixed with his rekindling desire. Tenderness for Diana Fontaine? It should have made him laugh. Instead, he spread a series of soft, hungry kisses over her face, coaxing her to give him her mouth.

"I want you again," he said, his voice turning thick. "God knows, you're exhausted and we both need some sleep, but I need—I just *need*, Diana."

She had to swallow to keep the tremor out of her voice, but the arms she slipped around his neck were strong and confident. "Then take me to bed and show me."

Sunlight streaked into the room through the opened blinds and the phone shrilled. Both were an irritation that had Diana grimacing the moment she woke up. She grabbed the receiver and shut her eyes against the offending glare.

Beside her, Adam took another sip of his coffee, enjoying the view as the sheet he'd finally covered them with slipped low on her back. It brought back all the hunger he thought had been sated hours ago.

That was a first. Women were not a priority in his life. Sure, he had the normal urges, but they didn't result in his waking up in a woman's bed, realizing he'd missed his tee off for the first time in almost three years, and being more interested in running his hands over the tantalizing curves of his sleeping companion's body. It had come as such a shock he'd bounded out of bed in search of the kitchen and some caffeine to clear his brain. But here he was, back again; and so were his unruly urges.

Unable to tell by the monotone responses who it was she was talking to, he went back to studying her bedroom, which—like the rest of the house—intrigued him, because it didn't match the image of the woman he thought he knew. It was less formal than he had expected, more homespun. The neutral sun-and-sand color scheme might be hell on the eyes when sleeping late, but it worked well to blend a contradictory decorating style. It took Adam a while to realize the odd combination of old and new furnishings were, like the knickknacks scattered about, a collection of sentimental favorites. The king-size brass bed might assure her a restful night's sleep, but the antique wicker armchair and chaise longue by the window might comfort in a different way if they'd come from her old bedroom, as he suspected. Photographs of herself and L.C., friends, maybe even distant relatives, covered side tables and dresser tops, interspersed with seashells and lifelike porcelain birds. Obviously she enjoyed being surrounded with reminders of those she cared about.

He thought of his own condominium closer to downtown, which he'd moved into upon selling the family homestead after his father's death. It had been decorated by one of the most popular interior designers in town, reflected his refined tastes and accommodated his busy life-style, but it contained no memories of the past. When he'd sold the house, he'd also sold everything in it at an auction. There were a few pictures, ones of himself and James as boys, but they were packed away in a box. Unlike Diana's, his memories were all tinged with bitterness and pain.

Finishing with her call, Diana hung up and buried her face in her pillow, emitting a low moan. Adam smiled in empathy. Three and a half hours hardly made up for a lost night's sleep.

"Have a sip of this," he suggested. "It'll help clear up the grogginess."

She whipped around, her eyes wide and startled. "Adam!"

Just as quickly a pink stain flooded her cheeks. Another first, he decided, pleased, though his smile turned wry. "Yes, I had a similar reaction when I awoke. This is one for the books, isn't it?"

"I only thought—you were so quiet, I thought you might have already left."

"Is that what you wanted?"

She could hear caution cool his voice and it made her want to reach out, to hold him. "No," she whispered. "It would have been awful."

He wanted to believe she meant that. The guileless appeal in her eyes, the sweet nostalgia he felt in this room made him believe that he could. "Here," he said, his voice gruff as he offered her the coffee again.

She sat up and took a tentative sip. Several hours old, it was worse than strong, but her second sip was greedier.

Adam hardly paid attention, caught up in the vision she made sitting before him like Copenhagen's famous mermaid. His lover. He'd marked her in his obsessive passion, he realized, rubbing his whiskers as his gaze fell to her breasts. Yet the only cry she made was when she'd reached her own climax.

"You didn't hurt me," she murmured, following his gaze and picking up on his thoughts. She set the coffee mug on the bed stand and lowered herself onto his chest, her fingers spreading to comb through gold and bronze curls. "It's just that I have sensitive skin."

"I noticed," he murmured, remembering how he could make her tremble with the slightest caress.

"I also bruise easily." She widened her exploration to trace a circle around his left nipple, then the right one. "Between the ages of five and ten I don't think there was a summer when my knees weren't covered with bandages. Rose always carried extra in her apron and..."

"What is it?" Adam asked, seeing the flash of grief in her eyes. Then he grimaced. Wrapping his arms more securely around her, he raised his head and kissed the tip of her nose. "I'm sorry. I never asked how she was doing."

"That was one of her daughters on the phone just now. She's stabilizing, and the doctors say if she continues to improve, they'll move her out of ICU later today."

"But that's good news. Why the frown?" he asked, combing his fingers through her hair and tucking it behind her ear.

"I'm letting her son sit in jail for the weekend, hoping it'll scare some sense into him. And I'm wondering how Rose is going to react when she hears that."

"I remember Martin saying it was auto theft. How old is he?"

"He turned eighteen last Wednesday, and no, this isn't his first arrest."

Nor was it her first time getting the boy out of trouble, Adam decided. "Tricky situation. You can probably get him off with a probation."

"I can get him off without one," she replied, though she was hardly pleased with that notion. "There's a technicality involved with precedents on record, but I'm not thrilled with the idea of using them."

"What? Is this the same Diana Fontaine who'll happily wear off the soles of a pair of Guccis to win another client's acquittal?"

"*Innocence* happens to be a motivating prerequisite," she said, using the same sardonic tone of voice. She should have known better than to expect him to understand. Disappointed, she began to lever herself off him, but before she could move away, he grasped her arms.

"Wait a minute. Go on and explain."

She was tempted to tell him to forget it. What they'd shared had been important to her, the most perfect experience she ever had with a man. She didn't want to ruin it by getting caught up with the same old tiresome arguments.

"I want to understand," he insisted, rubbing his thumbs in soothing circles over her taut skin.

Slowly she relaxed back against him, this time resting her chin on her folded hands. "The car was stolen while it was parked in front of an ice-cream parlor. The owner had run inside the store, leaving the keys in the car and the motor running."

Adam sighed. "I hear you: hit the car's owner with a negligence charge and he'll be happy he got it back in one piece and that the kid didn't run somebody over in the process."

"Which would make him an accessory to involuntary manslaughter." Diana shook her head. Sometimes she worried about a system that defended the criminal more than the victim. "Of course, I don't think jail is the answer to Leon's problem, but it's not fair that he should get off through this kind of loophole. What he did was wrong. He should be held accountable for that."

"Well, it's not exactly the Hilton he's spending the weekend at," Adam reminded her. "Maybe it'll be enough to straighten him out. Either way, it's not your place to exact punishment. Afterward, if he *does* manage to get off with barely a slap on the wrist, maybe you can try to get him some counseling."

"I suppose." Diana glanced at him from beneath her sable-brown lashes, a twinkle returning to her eyes. "Now who's doing a one-hundred-and-eighty-degree turnaround? Do you realize you just advised me on *behalf* of a client, instead of accusing me of near malpractice?"

"And you're never going to let me forget it, are you?"

"It's tempting," she murmured, stretching to place a kiss at the base of his throat where his pulse beat strongly. "But I suppose one good turn deserves another."

Desire began to churn in Adam again, but he banked it down, knowing there was more that had to be discussed. "And what about your father?" he asked quietly. "Have you come to terms with his condition?"

How did he...? "Martin," she whispered.

"Don't be hard on him. I didn't give him much choice. Actually, I'm surprised I hadn't heard about it earlier. But then it's probably an unspoken law not to mention anything about L. C. Fontaine to me," he acknowledged, wryly. He placed a finger beneath her chin to lift her head, then framed her face between his hands and ran his thumbs along the faint shadows under her eyes. "You fight your own battles, carry your own burdens and don't cry on anyone's shoulder, do you? It makes me wonder about how many other ways I was wrong about you."

"Maybe that's a subject better left alone for now," she replied, just as tentatively. "It would take more time than either of us has. As long as you're not sorry about what we shared."

"Is that all you want from me? One night?"

"It was hardly a night," she drawled, moving to get up.

He bolted upright and grabbed her. "You know what I mean," he snapped.

Diana tossed her hair back over her shoulder to meet his intense look. "What do you want from me?"

Angry that she achieved a coolness he couldn't, he swept her back across the mattress until she was pinned beneath him. It made no difference to tell himself that nothing could come of this. He knew they were all wrong for each other—two combustibles with trick fuses. But he also knew he'd never wanted like this before; never felt so alive as he did when she was in his arms.

"I want you to make me stop aching for you," he muttered.

Diana relaxed her grip on his wrists, ignored the sensible inner voice that reminded her she needed to get up. This, she told herself, was more important. It went

deeper than arousal; down to the foundations, beginnings—*theirs*.

"Never," she whispered, drawing him down to her.

Seven

Your Honor, considering the hour, I move that we table interviewing the next panel of potential jurors until after lunch."

Judge Lenore Canfield nodded to Diana. "At which time, counsels, I would appeal to you both to move things along a bit. Court is adjourned until two o'clock." She struck her gavel firmly, punctuating her displeasure and concluding the session.

Diana exhaled in relief and—after giving Alice Porter a reassuring smile as she was escorted back to her cell—began shoving papers into her briefcase. What a morning. Two groups of jury candidates interviewed so far, and only one person had been selected as acceptable by both the defense *and* the prosecution.

"In my office—ten minutes," Adam murmured as he stepped over to her table.

She cast him a droll look. "Should I come armed, or is this an amicable meeting with the opposition?"

"A good strategist never tips his hand. Nine and a half minutes."

Diana repressed a smile—and the urge to glance over her shoulder to watch him walk away. If she was smart, she told herself, she would go back to her own office, send out for some Chinese food, and try to juggle eight hours of work into the three she now had. But when she stepped into the elevator minutes later, it wasn't the lobby button she pushed.

With nothing resolved and everything more complex than ever, she and Adam were plunging into a blazing affair. What with the Porter case beginning, the timing couldn't be worse. They both needed to keep their wits about them, especially since the press was becoming a habitual presence in the courthouse lobby. They didn't need the added pressure of having their relationship—fragile as it was—speculated upon and held under a microscope by the media and the public. Besides, it would only serve to finish turning the case into a three-ring circus.

Yet her heart raced with excitement as she breezed by Muriel's unoccupied desk, tapped on Adam's door and walked in. Bad timing or not, this past week, with their impromptu visits and stolen hours, had been incredible. Not even as a teenager experiencing infatuation for the first time, had she ever felt this depth of exhilaration. And it was simply to *see* him, to spend a few quiet moments alone with him before they went on with their respective schedules. That made it all the more remarkable.

But two steps into his office, she stopped. He wasn't there. She glanced at her watch and frowned. Didn't he say ten minutes? She'd made it in seven.

"What an appealing sight," he murmured behind her, nudging the door closed with his foot. "Were you really disappointed not to find me behind my desk?"

"No. Annoyed," she replied, setting her briefcase in the nearest chair. But when he drew her into his arms, she went willingly. Dressed in an oyster-gray suit with a red-and-gray striped tie, he looked every bit the power broker he was destined to be in Austin, or maybe even Washington. Yet in his eyes she could see the admiration and unquenched desire of the charismatic man she'd spent yesterday afternoon with, listening to Chopin and making love. "I said to myself, 'See there, Fontaine, it's been barely three weeks and already he's taking it for granted that you'd wait for him.'"

Her glib reply disappointed him, and what had been meant to be a tender kiss became a punishing one. At least in this, he decided, as her lips softened and her body melted against his, he knew she couldn't hide her true feelings. When he raised his head again, he was satisfied to see he'd erased all signs of the cool, collected woman who'd just challenged him to another verbal fencing match.

"Now tell me what you *really* thought," he demanded, his gaze wandering restlessly over her face.

"I thought..." She paused to catch her breath. "I thought how empty the office feels without you in it."

It was more than he'd expected. Moved, the only response he could think of was to hand her the flower he'd been hiding behind his back. It was a rosebud he picked up on impulse while driving into the city this morning. Pink and perfect, it reminded him of her lips.

"Adam—it's lovely."

He watched as she lifted it close to capture its delicate scent, brushed it against her cheek. "A full dozen would probably have been more impressive," he murmured, his voice gruff.

"But hardly as eloquent. Thank you." She raised her head to give him a featherlight kiss. "Do you realize this is the first gift you've given me? I'm going to press it and put it into my scrapbook."

He liked the idea of that. Having given away so much of his and the family's history, he liked to think that something would remain, and that someone would think of him specifically. He slipped his fingers under her chin to raise her head again, and this time when he kissed her, the tenderness came easily.

"Let's lock the door and make love on the couch for the rest of the day," he murmured against her lips.

"We have to be back in court at two."

"Until two, then."

"And what happens when Muriel returns and wonders why the door's locked?"

He uttered a low groan. "You really know how to cool a guy off."

"And here I hoped you had a viable solution."

"None that will change the fact that she *will* be back in a minute with a memo I've got to sign." Still, he made no movement to release her. It felt too good. She'd looked so untouchable in the courtroom, so competent in her powder-blue suit and navy blouse, and it reassured him to discover that it was a facade, to feel her body reacting to his as helplessly as his was reacting to hers.

"Now, what are you thinking?" Diana asked, fascinated by the warmth radiating from his eyes.

"I'm fantasizing about you wearing those pearls—and nothing else."

Her answering laugh was low and seductive. "Maybe you'd better reconsider locking the door, after all."

Of course he couldn't and didn't, but because he knew he needed something to get him through the rest of the day, he took her mouth under his and showed her with his lips and tongue what he really wanted from her. Her immediate response—unbridled passion that went from a simmer to a boil in mere heartbeats—stunned him no less than it had the first time he experienced it.

"No more," he rasped, finally sliding his hands from her hips to her shoulders to put her out of temptation's reach. "Damn it, woman, you're a lethal brew."

No less shaken, Diana backed away before she lost herself to him completely, but a teasing light danced in her eyes. "This is much more pleasant than the scene I anticipated. I was certain you'd invited me up here to complain about what went on in the courtroom this morning."

He lifted his gaze toward the ceiling, remembering the contest of wills that had ended in stalemate, remembering the annoyance and grudging admiration he'd experienced for her as she read his strategy and nullified it. "Complain?" He dipped his hands into his pockets and circled around her to go to his desk. "There were moments when I wanted to do more than complain."

Grinning, Diana slid onto the right corner, the only spot not covered with files. "Oh, I can imagine. Especially when I challenged that bricklayer you accepted and had him disqualified for cause."

"Cause? I heard you call him a Neanderthal under your breath; just because a guy's divorced and prefers beer joints to mortgage payments doesn't mean he's another Carl Porter."

"Aha! So you do agree Porter was a louse."

"Maybe he was, but that doesn't justify his old lady turning him into a lead paperweight. And while we're at it, you can forget about trying to fill the panel with all those career women. Most of them were so battle fatigued they looked like they'd approve of emasculating any male over sixteen."

"Careful—your chauvinism is showing," she warned, wagging her finger at him.

He stood behind his desk and gave her a narrow-eyed look. "A male chauvinist wouldn't get involved with a stubborn, infuriating lady attorney, no matter how sexy he found her."

"A true trial by fire, eh?"

He leaned toward her, placing one hand on the desk for balance. "Certainly not for the fainthearted."

Diana smiled as she reached out and closed her fingers around his tie. Gently she drew him toward her, closer until their noses touched, then she subtly stroked hers against his. "Kiss me and I'll forgive you for that crack."

He wanted to do more than kiss her. He wanted to fill himself with her, lose himself in her softness and her scent. She gave so generously, and his needs went deep. But as he tilted his head and inched closer, a knock at the door pulled a groan of disgust, not pleasure, from him.

He dropped back into his chair and closed his eyes. "*Come in* . . . at your own risk," he added under his breath.

"Well, you needn't sound so grumpy," Muriel muttered, entering. "You're the one who said this couldn't wait until after ... Hi there, Diana."

"Hello, Muriel." Diana gave her a benign smile, while dangling a navy pump from her toes. "Nice to see you again."

"You, too. Say, guess who I saw in church yesterday? Sister Mary Pauline."

Oh, God, Adam groaned silently. "Muriel. The memo?"

She gave him a resentful look and handed it over, then turned back to Diana. "I had no idea we belonged to *' same church. Isn't that ironic? She saw the report on the news earlier this month about you representing Mrs. Porter and asked me if I'd seen you lately."

"She's a sweet person. How's your sister's bursitis?"

"Not well at all. Her senior citizens' bowling team is in contention for the league championship and she's missed two practices in the past week."

Having proofed and signed the memorandum, Adam tried to hand it back, only to be ignored. "Excuse me," he interrupted at last. Pale blue eyes drilled into Muriel. "I thought you were in a hurry to go to lunch?"

She snatched the sheet of paper out of his hands, her gaze equally frigid. After saying goodbye to Diana, she stalked to the door, intoned "Eight months," and closed it with excessive care.

Diana ran a finger along her left eyebrow. "You know, for a man who aspires to hold a higher public office, you show an alarming talent for encouraging defection."

"What defection? The first day I walked into this place she point-blank told me she voted for the other guy."

"What happens in eight months?"

"She retires . . . or the building collapses from stress damage caused by the barbs we've flung at each other over the past three years. Whichever comes first."

Unable to contain it any longer, Diana laughed and shook her head. "You're going to miss her when she's gone."

"Oil and vinegar, my dear."

"And which are you?" she teased.

A growl rumbled deep in his throat. "Have dinner with me and I'll give you a list of subjects I prefer to talk about."

She was about to accept—the thought of sharing a romantic dinner with him in a restaurant was already a favorite fantasy of hers—then gnawed at her lower lip. "Oh, Adam. Do you think it's wise?"

"In case you haven't noticed, wisdom has eluded me since the morning I showed up at your house."

"Very gallant," she murmured, watching him rise and circle the desk to come to her. "But I think we should discuss this seriously. Is this a good time for our personal relationship to become public? The fact that we're both on this case is already earning it more attention than is helpful."

Adam picked up her hand and idly ran his thumb over the smooth skin. "It's not going to be much of a relationship if I can only invite you out between cases."

His tone was light, but Diana caught the slight tensing of his mouth muscles. He cares, she thought, feeling a warmth seep through her. He may not like it very much yet, but it's more than lust; he cares. "Come to my place for dinner," she murmured, lacing her fingers through his.

"You cooked yesterday."

"I didn't poison you, did I?"

"What I mean is, we'll both be in court until who knows when. It's not fair to ask you to cook on top of that."

Diana ran her finger up and down the lapel of his jacket. "I can raid the freezer. Rose always keeps it stocked with all kinds of things. Even if she decides to retire, it'll take me weeks to use it all. She makes a mean lasagna...."

"Lasagna it is, then," Adam murmured, raising their joined hands to his lips and kissing hers. "I'll bring the wine. By the way, how is Rose doing?"

"Better. She's already worrying that I might be destroying her well-ordered kitchen."

"And Leon?"

Diana sighed. "Well, time will tell. I *did* get him into a counseling group and he is concerned about his mother, but he told me in no uncertain terms that if I knew what was good for me, I'd 'stay out of his face.'"

"Obviously a young man of unrefined tastes," he drawled. His phone signaled a call. He shot it an impatient look before returning his attention to Diana. "Now about Judge Canfield's polite rebuke this morning. What do you say we talk compromise?"

The phone kept buzzing and Diana raised an eyebrow questioningly, but when Adam continued to ignore it she shrugged. "Considering you didn't want me to take this case at all, I think that's very indulgent of you."

"Since your decision's already made, I'm doing my best to be pragmatic. You stop trying to sneak in your radical feminists and I'll—oh, for crying out loud," he muttered, grabbing for the phone.

Diana's frustration almost matched his. Interruptions and conflicting schedules were proving to be as big an obstacle to their being together as anything else. The price of being a success, she mused, while adjusting her pearl stud earrings.

"Oh, no. What?" she asked, recognizing the look on his face as he hung up.

"The mayor wants a meeting tonight. That investigative report about downtown crime started running in this morning's paper and he wants me to be able to make a rebuttal on tomorrow's evening news." He gave her a crooked smile. "It looks like it's my turn to stand you up."

"Maybe someone is trying to tell us something." She pushed herself off the desk and headed for her briefcase.

Adam caught up with her at the door, trapping her against it by bracing his hands on either side of her. "Diana—we're good together."

"I know it." But that didn't offset all the negatives weighing down the other side of the scale. She lifted a hand to his cheek. "If you think you'll get out early, why don't you come over afterward."

"Would you mind if I stopped at my place first and got a change of clothes?"

Such a little thing, and probably thought of only out of practicality, yet Diana's heart sprouted wings. Even last night he'd gone home. "I'd like that," she told him quietly.

He shifted the hand at his cheek to his lips and pressed a kiss in her palm. "Then I'll see you back in court at two—where we'll do our best to placate Judge

Canfield and each other by choosing practical men and women who will inspire us with their ability to be model arbiters.''

''And just the other day I was reading about orators being a lost breed,'' she murmured, tongue in cheek.

''Wait until you hear my closing remarks.''

The subtle challenge had her straightening her back. Lovers or enemies, they thrived on competition—on what they instinctively knew they could expect from each other: their best effort. Diana respected him for that, even as she wanted to make him swallow that confident smile on his face.

''Wasn't it Kipling who wrote, 'You haf too much Ego in your Cosmos'?'' she mused.

''Mmm-hmm.'' He bent to place a nipping kiss near her ear. ''And I believe it was the wolf in 'Little Red Riding Hood' who said, 'The better to catch you with, my dear.'''

Laughing, Diana gently pushed him away. ''Let me out of here. I really do have to get back to my office.''

''Later?''

She glanced back, a promise in her eyes. ''Later.''

Half the office was gone for lunch, Diana discovered upon arriving with her own meal. Workmen were taking advantage of the lull in traffic to lay the plastic runners Oscar had ordered, while he stood in the doorway of his office, somber in his role as overseer. After exchanging greetings with him, Diana continued on toward Andrea's desk.

''Ah, the smell of progress.'' She sighed.

Andy, golden tanned from her vacation, wrinkled her nose. ''Smells like poly-what's-is to me. How'd it go this morning?''

"One down, eleven to go."

The younger woman pursed her lips in a silent whis-tle. "Wish I could have been there."

"Lenore was *not* amused. I'm sure I'm going to get a lecture at the next association meeting." The sparkle in Diana's eyes indicated she still thought it was worth it. "Court resumes at two, so be sure to throw me out of here by one-thirty at the latest, okay?"

"You bet. By the way, Mr. Fontaine is still here."

Thanking her, Diana put her briefcase in her office and, taking her lunch sack with her, went to seek him out. His office was at the end of the hall, dubbed the Throne Room by the staff who admired L. C. Fontaine but were in awe of him, as well. Diana found him there dictating a letter to his longtime secretary, Elaine.

L.C.'s eyes lit when he saw her and he made a flour-ishing movement with his hand to the dainty, silver-haired woman who sat facing him. "Er, you know the rest, my best wishes to the family and so on."

"Uh-oh. Sounds like an endorsement letter to me," Diana teased, winking to Elaine as the elderly woman rose and smiled in greeting.

"Something like that. Old Crenshaw's grandson is fresh from law school and looking for a job. We can't use him, but I thought I'd send him over to Perkins, Ross. Come sit down and tell me how the clash of the Titans went this morning. You don't look any worse for wear, so I'll assume you held your own. What's in the bag? I smell sweet and sour. How did you know I've been craving some?"

"You crave everything that Walters won't prepare for you," Diana murmured, exchanging indulgent glances with his departing secretary. She ignored the intention-ally uncomfortable English Regency chairs facing the massive mahogany desk and circled it to perch herself on a finely polished corner. "He told me he found a crumpled napkin from—now, how did he put it?—one of those 'barbecue establishments' in your pocket the other day. Shame on you."

"I wanted some ribs and they have the best in town," he grumbled. "It's a wonder I haven't grown long ears and a cottontail, what with all the carrots and greens he's been feeding me. The only time he cooks a decent meal is when he knows you're coming."

"He's only following instructions, and you know the roughage is supposed to be good for you. Now stop complaining and I'll make an exception this time and share my lunch with you."

Mollified, L.C. sat back, crossing his arms over the vest of his gray striped suit. "So it went well, did it?"

"I feel like I've just gone through the bar exam again, but then I have a feeling he does, too."

Her father slapped the arm of his chair in pleasure. "Tell me about it."

She did while emptying the sack and spreading their meal on his blotter. When she was through, she dipped a tiny shrimp in the Styrofoam cup of sweet-and-sour sauce and popped it into her mouth.

"Well, I can't say I'm pleased that you took this case myself," her father mused, reaching for an egg roll, "but it sounds as though you're in control. As a matter of fact, I don't know when I've seen you looking quite so—"

"Don't you dare," she warned, emphasizing each word with a wave of her minidrumstick.

"I was only going to say content."

"Uh-huh." She bit off a piece of chicken and chewed, watching him through narrowed eyes. "I've told you before, I've never meddled in your private life and I'd appreciate the same consideration."

"How could you? You were either too young or away at school." When she dismissed the technicality with a slight lift of one shoulder, he scowled and took an inordinate interest in studying what was in the rest of the containers. "Doesn't matter, anyway," he said at last. "I already know you've been seeing him."

The last bite of chicken almost stuck in her throat. "How?" she croaked.

"I called you the other evening...and called...and called. Since I know it's not your habit to leave the phone off the hook I sent the General over to make sure you were all right. He came back fifteen minutes later with the license number of a Mercedes in your driveway. A few phone calls later, I knew what I wanted to know."

Diana shut her eyes. She should be furious with him, but she knew it would be a waste of energy. He was never going to change.

"Really, Father."

"Just tell me this—are you happy?"

To buy time, she dropped the chicken bone onto a plastic lid and wiped her hands with one of the napkins still in the bag. Happy? Did that explain the roller coaster her emotions were riding between euphoria and depression? She knew that when she looked into a mirror these days, her skin had a certain glow, her eyes a deeper warmth. But it also bothered her that when they talked, it was about the present, never about the past, never about family and childhood things that normal couples discuss in that tentative way of linking together their lives. Their past was already linked in an irrevocable, wrong way. And though she told herself it was still too soon to worry about it, she knew the way everything else between them was happening so quickly, something had to give. Soon.

"I much prefer being given flowers than being read the riot act, if that's what you mean," she replied, thinking about the rose she'd tucked away in her brief-case.

"No, that's not what I want to hear." L.C. made a disgruntled sound. "You're not going to tell me a blessed thing, are you? Going to let me read about it in the paper like a perfect stranger."

"We're trying our best to keep it out of the paper."

"Humph. Good luck."

"And if or when there's something to tell, you'll be the second to know," she continued, ignoring that.

"Second! Just goes to show you how things change. There was a time when I'd be first."

She knew he was only teasing her, but she reached across and covered his hand with her own. "Dad, in some ways you'll always be number one."

L.C. looked up at his only child, pride warming his eyes, and patted her hand with his free one. "I know, baby. I know."

He was late and she was waiting—curled up on the couch with the small mountain of briefs she'd brought home, but waiting. Though she'd made a good dent in the stack, for the past hour she'd been glancing at her watch and gazing off to daydream more than she'd been reading. If she didn't straighten up her act soon, she was going to fall hopelessly behind in her work.

If he wasn't coming, he would call, she reminded herself. He was particularly considerate in that way. *But suppose there was an accident?* She slipped off her glasses and stared into space. He could be in an ambulance and on his way to a hospital this very minute, and if he were unable to speak, no one would know to tell her. She could turn on the news tomorrow morning the way a virtual stranger would....

"Enough!" she muttered, exasperated with herself. She shut the file she was working on and dumped it along with her glasses onto the glass-topped coffee table. Rising from the couch, she slid her hands deep into the pockets of her burgundy caftan and stepped over to the bay window.

Illuminated by the inside lights, her neighbor's gray cat sat in its favorite night roost—her deck chair. It gave her an insouciant glance before returning to its bedtime wash. The scene soothed Diana, though her perfectionist's eye envisioned the same setting with more flowers. But she had little time to fiddle with flowers, just as she had no time to give a pet of her own the attention it deserved.

Beyond the deck a distant flash of light drew her gaze. Far off at sea a storm was brewing, and lightning illuminated the indigo sky with splashes of pink and purple. That particular storm was too far south to do them any good, but perhaps there were others forming. They needed the rain.

The sound of a car in her driveway had her spinning around, but this time it was relief, not nerves, that had her heart pounding. She let out a pent-up breath and hurried to the door.

He was tired and had the beginnings of a headache, but when he rounded the bend in the sidewalk and saw her standing there, both were blocked out by pleasure. Here was the Diana who enchanted him: barefoot, her hair a slightly mussed cloud of pale gold, a smile of welcome on her lips. His own curved readily.

"Hi," she said, closing the door behind him and bolting it for the night. "I was beginning to wonder if they were going to work you all night."

"Me, too."

She watched him toss his garment bag over the back of the couch. "Can I get you something? A drink? Something to eat?"

"Just this," he replied, slipping an arm around her waist and drawing her against him. He buried his other hand in her hair. "God, just this."

His mouth was demanding, his hunger too sharp to temper with soft words and softer caresses, but Diana didn't care. It was his honesty she wanted, and if that honesty reflected an almost primitive need, then so be it.

Yet she couldn't stop her body from trembling in response to the flood of sensations he wrung from her. Out of necessity she clung to him. Out of desire her touch became as demanding as his.

"They gave us reports to read and all I could see was your face," he muttered, pressing his lips to her throat. "They fed us coffee and sandwiches, and all I could taste was you."

"I worried you might have had a wreck." She caught her breath as he slid his hand from thigh to breast, molding what he already knew so well, torturing her with a promise of pleasure to come. "It was driving me crazy."

"Good. Misery loves company."

"Adam!" She laughed softly, nuzzling his ear.

"Let's go to bed, Diana. I need you."

Defenseless against that, she took his hand and led him down the hallway, ignoring the lights that needed to be turned off, the locks that needed to be rechecked.

The bedroom was dark, the bed already turned back in invitation. To Adam it was as welcoming as coming to his own bed. More, because she was with him. He slipped off his jacket and reached for his tie.

"Let me," she whispered, already brushing away his hands to untangle the silk knot. Stretching, she touched her lips to his. She had needs, too; the need to explore again the realm of pleasure only he could bring her; the need to hear him say her name in that moment before sanity slipped out of his reach. The need to simply give. When she heard the deep sound of approval he made as she slid her hands into his opened shirt, she knew all that would be satisfied—and more.

Her lips touched skin and felt heat. She cooled him with the tip of her tongue and felt the fierce pounding of his heart, heard the catch in his breathing. Power rushed through her. He was hers. The knowledge was thrilling. She'd never wanted a man body and soul before; work had been her obsession. Now she understood why. She had been saving that part of herself for him.

Adam sensed a difference, yet knew no name for it. He didn't even know if it came from within her or himself. But as her fingers trailed down to loosen his belt, he realized it hardly mattered from where it came, only that it was real.

Her touch was light, her methods quick. A buckle here, a snap there and soon there wasn't an inch of him that wasn't hers to explore at will. But instead, she gently nudged him back on the bed, then stepped back to draw the long zipper on her caftan downward. She smiled, seeing his eyes probe the parted robe, eager for the sight of her, and she didn't keep him waiting. Reaching up, she drew the robe from her shoulders and let warm satin abandon her in a long caress.

Cooler night air licked at her, creating a tingling intensified by his sweeping gaze. "I want you," she whispered, lowering herself over him. "I want your hands and your mouth—" Her voice broke as he took possession of her breast and suckled deeply. "I want your heat pouring into me," she moaned, pressing her lips to his. "Love me, Adam. Make love to me as you've never loved anyone before."

"Diana." He rolled her onto her back, claiming her mouth before she could catch her breath. His tongue drove deep to meet with hers. Madness. She lured him so effortlessly to madness, stripping him of what was left of his civilized side. Drums pounding in his head, he dragged his mouth down to her other breast. Fever burning in his blood, he slipped his fingers into her richer source of heat and raced her toward her first peak.

But it wasn't enough. He soon wondered if anything was.

Again and again they rolled over the bed and, each time, they took each other to a higher peak, until their bodies were drenched and throbbing with tension.

"I once told you I didn't want this," he ground out, straddling her across his hips. As she lifted her hands to rake her hair back, he slid his hands over her sweat-slicked breasts, drawing a helpless shudder from her. "I lied. I wanted you from the moment I first saw you at that party. Before. I've got years of hunger to quench, Diana."

"I know," she whispered, bending to kiss him softly. "I'll take care of it."

Slowly she moved over him, shivering with ecstasy as he groaned and surged inside her. She didn't wince when he shifted his hands to a biting hold of her hips; she merely smiled and continued rocking, her pace a retreat from frenzy, but no less intense.

And slowly she lowered herself to him, until their heartbeats pounded as one, their breaths and lips joined, and their eyes guiding them to one pleasure.

"Now," she whispered, sensing the moment approach like a surging wave.

Adam felt it, too, heard the roar reverberate in his ears and the power of it swell in him until he thought he might explode. But what sent him over the edge was Diana's soft sob, and the barely audible words—*I love you.*

Love....I love you.... You. He played with the words over and over again in his mind. They sounded right and yet he wondered. Were they throwaways? Were they merely a moment taken out of context when what she really meant was, *I desire you?*

Beside him, Diana shifted and pressed a kiss to his chest. "Are you asleep?"

"Not yet." He lifted a strand of her hair and admired its silvery-gold color in the dim light. "I want to take a shower first."

"Me, too. We can conserve water by showering together."

"I haven't heard anything about a water shortage."

"That's because there isn't one. Yet," she murmured, turning onto her stomach to grin at him. "But it makes for good practice."

Adam ran his index finger down the length of her nose. "We always get into trouble in there. What are you trying to do, maim me?"

Her soft chuckle ended on a weary sigh. "It'll be just a shower, I promise. I'm too tired for anything else myself. But I am happy you're here," she added, pressing her cheek to his heart. "Because I know that no sooner will I close my eyes than it'll be time to get up and the whole cycle will start all over again, and I want to hold on to the moment for as long as I can."

Adam stroked her hair, thinking it was the same for him. "What did you do when you left my office this morning?"

"I went back to mine and ate lunch out of Styrofoam containers while dreaming of dinners by candlelight." She held back mentioning L.C., wondering if it was the right time.

"I wonder if I'd have been able to resist you if I'd sensed the romantic streak in you sooner," he murmured, amused.

"Probably." She combed her fingers through the damp golden curls covering his chest. "You have an enormous talent for being pigheaded."

"Don't waste all your compliments at once."

"Pigheaded, but gorgeous. How's that?"

"It needs some work."

Diana laughed, delighted that they could relax together like this. "Tell me about your meeting. Did it go well?"

His hesitation lasted only an instant, but long enough for her to notice. Seeing her disappointment, he caught her chin and forced her to look at him. "You don't drop habits overnight, okay?"

"I'm not asking you to expose any secrets," she replied just as quietly. "I only wanted to learn about the other parts of your life apart from the courtroom."

He knew that. Sunday they'd spent part of the day talking about favorite things—food, wine, music. He'd called her a musical garbage disposal and she'd called him a cultural snob. He hadn't laughed so much in years.

"The meeting didn't go well or badly," he murmured, after another moment. His mouth tightened with remembered frustration. "The mayor was looking for an excuse, when what he needs to be focusing on is the source for why the crime figures are on the rise— which everyone knows is drugs."

"Did you tell him that?"

"Yeah."

"And?"

"He brushed it aside by making a crack about my political aspirations."

Diana made a sound of commiseration. "I'm sorry."

"It's part of the power game," he said, dismissing it. "His career is about over and it gives him a thrill to put me, as the new kid on the block, in my place."

Thinking about that and his ambitions, Diana asked him which office he wanted to run for next. "Or do you want to be district attorney for another term? It's hard to believe that this time next year you'll already have to have your campaign under way."

"Don't remind me," he groaned. "And no, I haven't decided. Rumor has it that the attorney general's spot will be available, but the more I think about it, the more I believe I'd do better to have another term here under my belt before I start looking toward Austin."

Diana tried not to show her relief, but didn't quite succeed. They were beginning to get close; she dreaded thinking he might leave, dreaded wondering whether they might lose that closeness.

"Was that a sigh of disappointment I heard? Don't tell me now that you've had your way with me you've lost interest?"

She lowered her lashes to hide her true feelings and sniffed, "You always did have a disgustingly obvious way of fishing for a compliment."

"How would you know unless you kept close watch?"

"Adam!" She burst into laughter as he rolled her beneath him and began tickling her with his day's growth of whiskers.

"Confess, woman!"

Instead, she wrapped her arms around his neck and gave him a kiss that soon made them both forget what it was they'd been talking about. Finally Adam touched his lips to her forehead before resting his there to gaze warmly into her eyes.

"Tell me what your schedule looks like for the rest of the week—outside of those delightful hours you'll be spending in court with me, that is."

"They're probably no less dreadful than yours. Tomorrow evening I'm giving a lecture, Thursday I have a meeting and Friday I promised I'd attend a dinner at the Prescotts'. Martin's older brother is getting married and I've known them all for ages."

"A likely story," Adam grumbled. "Looks like I won't get to see you again until the weekend. No, wait . . . Wednesday is good for me, too."

Diana moistened her lips with the tip of her tongue. "I'm not free on Wednesday. That's when I have dinner and a visit with L.C. But look, it's nothing formal or private," she added quickly, sensing a change in him already. "I'm sure he'd enjoy having you come along."

"You must be joking."

"Excuse me?"

Adam rolled onto his side to rest on one elbow and study her. His expression was no less incredulous than hers. "You're serious. You actually want me to go to L. C. Fontaine's house, eat his food and make small talk?"

"He's my father, Adam, not one of the Borgias," she said, trying to make a joke out of it. But she could see by his expression that he didn't see a lot of difference in the two. Hurt came quickly, and along with it an awful dread. "I thought you were coming to terms with all that. I thought that now you and I . . ." Her words died off because she was already beginning to feel as if she'd made a terrible mistake.

"Was that the catch?" he asked sharply. "Take me, but my father comes along as part of the package?"

Diana slowly sat up but resisted the urge to pull the sheet over herself, though his scathing glance made her feel her nakedness and destroyed the lingering happiness they had just shared. "I don't deserve that," she replied with quiet dignity. "I wouldn't sell myself in a courtroom and I certainly wouldn't sell myself in bed."

"But it all boils down to you expecting me to ignore my own beliefs if I want you, doesn't it?"

"No! But—" She shook her head in frustration. "Adam, this is ridiculous. If we want to be together, doesn't it follow that we should do what we can to work out those things that we disagree on?"

"Everything but that." The ice in his voice matched that in his eyes. "Have dinner with him. Be with him when you must, but leave me out of that part of your life. I don't need it and I *don't* want it."

His cruelty sliced at her brutally. Her eyes burned. Her chest ached. "Obviously we have a difference of opinion about what kind of relationship we're striving for," she managed in a ghostly voice. "I asked you before what you wanted from me. I'm asking you again."

"I want *you*. Isn't that enough?"

She wanted it to be, but she'd told him she loved him, and to her, love meant sharing the bad along with the good. It meant sharing everything, including the past, for better or worse.

"I guess not," she whispered numbly. "Because I know I can look at you and see the man, as well as the son and know it doesn't make any difference to me. But you can't do that, can you?"

Adam felt the clutch of panic like sharp claws but forced himself to ignore it. "Don't make this into an ultimatum, Diana."

"I don't have to. You already did that for me."

He sat up and, without another word, reached for his clothes. She reached for a pillow and clutched it tightly against the pain tearing at her. Outside, the wind was picking up—a storm was coming. The one inside had run its course.

Adam slipped on his shirt but didn't bother buttoning it. Temper already had him burning up. He snatched up his jacket and tie, then turned to look at her. God, she was beautiful. Even now, he ached for her. But she asked for too damned much.

"You spoke of love," he said, his voice heavy with bitterness, "and you spoke of not selling yourself. But it seems to me there's a pretty hefty price tag attached to your affections, sweetheart."

For a moment all she could do was stare at him. Then she got up and walked into the bathroom, carefully closing the door behind her. Moments later she heard the faint sound of the front door opening and closing.

Numb, she groped for the bathroom light switch. The bright glare hurt her eyes and accelerated the throbbing collecting at her temples. Blindly she reached for the medicine cabinet and aspirin. Her trembling hands knocked something else off the shelf and into the washbasin. It was the disk containing her birth-control pills, the last of her prescription. They reminded her of her last examination and the doctor's gentle reminder that it was getting close to the time for some major decisions.

Major decisions. Well, she'd just made one, hadn't she?

With the disk clutched in her hand, Diana crumpled to the carpeted floor and burst into tears.

Eight

Days passed in a blur of excessive work and too much caffeine. By Thursday Diana had a new appreciation of what numb meant. During luncheon recess she literally stepped into an elevator with Martin and didn't recognize him. When they reached the lobby of the courthouse, he took her arm and led her to the restaurant across the street. Though the place was a favorite, she protested all the way up to the reception desk.

"But I'm not hungry!" she said under her breath.

"And I'm not buying that," he replied, glaring back at her. "Look at you; you're about to drop from low blood sugar or something. If I let you get into your car, you'd probably pass out before you got three blocks. What the hell's the matter with you, Diana?"

"Probably a spring cold."

"Try again. In that respect, you're as healthy as a horse."

Too tired to argue with him, Diana simply followed the hostess who led them to their table. At least it was dark here, she told herself as she took her seat. There was an unspoken agreement among the attorneys and judges who frequented the establishment that discouraged cross-table socializing unless it was invited, and Diana—spotting several colleagues—was grateful for that, as well. But when Martin ordered them both cocktails, she sent him a look that warned him he'd about pushed her too far.

"Don't bother telling me you don't want it or that you have to go back into court. If you don't get some color back into your cheeks, the only place you'll be going is to a hospital."

"As a matter of fact, I don't have to be back in court until tomorrow morning."

That brought his head up. "You've got your jury."

She inclined her head, knowing as Martin did that all across town, bets were being paid and collected. "Tomorrow we face off for round two."

"For a while there, I thought you were going for some kind of record."

So did Diana. After Adam had left her Monday night, it had seemed that all the old suspicions returned and that neither of them could agree on a jury candidate for Tuesday. Wednesday—only because of another reprimand from Judge Canfield—was somewhat better, and this morning they filled the final two slots.

"I'd have thought the improved relationship between you two would—uh-oh."

Diana looked from Martin to the direction of his gaze in time to see Adam walk in with a blonde. Not just any blonde, she realized a moment later, but the one in the photograph on his desk. Before she could look away, she found her eyes locked with his, and the temperature in the room felt as if it had dropped ten degrees.

"Now I get it," Martin murmured, as the other couple was shown to a table across the room.

"Good. Then you'll understand when I warn you that I don't want to talk about it." A waitress arrived with their drinks and, having decided she wanted the wine, after all, Diana took a long sip.

"We could leave," Martin told her, concerned at the way her hand was shaking.

The smile she gave him was brittle. "Why? I'm perfectly all right. He's with his friend, I'm with mine. Life goes on."

"I wonder what brought her back to town?"

"Oh, I imagine a simple phone call."

Martin reached across the table and covered her hand with his. "Di, don't do this to yourself. What can I do to help?"

"Nothing." She squeezed his hand before withdrawing. "I got myself into this, and I'll recover. Now let's order," she added with forced cheerfulness. No one would see her humiliation. Her heart might break, but it would remain her secret how deep the pain went. If she were to continue with this case, continue working in this city, her pride demanded it.

Adam understood pride. He was having his own battle with it as he and Kendall Manning sat down at their table.

In the last three days he'd watched the shadows darken under Diana's eyes, watched her grow as pale as a wraith. He knew he didn't look much better, but his concern had been for her. The little fool was obviously pushing herself beyond reasonable limits. Yet pride kept him silent, just as it had made him respond to her cool nod just now with an equally curt acknowledgement.

"I'm glad I decided to stop by your office," Kendall said, interrupting his thoughts. "We get to see each other so rarely that this was an opportunity I decided was too good to pass up."

Her radiant smile made it easier for him to summon one of his own. "I'm glad you did, too. This is exactly the break I've been needing."

"I thought as much." Her green eyes scanned his face, seeing lines that weren't there when they'd last visited. "Rough schedule?"

"Somewhat. I'd rather hear about yours. Did you say you and Matt were visiting with the Ortegas all weekend?"

"Mmm. Braden had us fly down and he's driving in Saturday. He and Frank are going to start on that addition to the house Ginger's been asking for. It'll probably take all summer to finish, but at the rate their new baby boy is growing it won't be soon enough."

"Well, that's terrific. Keep me posted about when you're in town and maybe I can get out there to visit."

"But I'd better warn you that if you do come, you might find yourself with a hammer in your hand," she teased.

Adam shrugged and picked up his menu. "Only until they realize the only nail I ever hammered in my life was to hang up my diplomas in my office."

Kendall chuckled and reached for her own menu, her gaze wandering around the room. A moment later she shifted in her seat and cleared her throat. "Umm— Adam, can I ask you something?"

"Sure."

"You know the attractive couple sitting across the room? The ones you nodded to as we came in? I think I remember the man from the old days—he's an attorney, right? But I don't think I recognize the woman, and the way she's staring holes into me, I keep getting the feeling that I should."

"It's the company you're keeping," he replied flatly. He closed his menu, set it aside and met Kendall's perplexed gaze. "That's Diana Fontaine."

A waiter came to bring them their drinks and take their meal orders, giving Kendall time to recuperate. But as soon as he left, she still had to take a deep gulp of her ice tea.

"*That's* the virago you've been describing all these months? Adam, she's gorgeous!"

"I'm aware of that," he muttered, taking a healthy swallow of his Scotch.

"And jealous."

He shot her a quick look. Too late, he discovered he'd been tricked. "Leave it alone, honey," he warned, his voice tender but firm.

Kendall reached across the table to touch his arm. "No way. I care about you, and it doesn't take a genius to see you're both hurting, so why don't you save us both a lot of hot air and tell me what's happened since we last talked."

"We tried to make things work out and they didn't, okay?"

"It's a start."

Adam took another sip. It wasn't easy. He'd spent so much of his life without confidants that just anticipating the thought of opening up that much made him feel awkward. And yet, what did he have to lose? Could anything make him feel more miserable than he felt now? And hadn't Kendall already proved her friendship to him?

"It goes back years," he began slowly. "Our fathers were boyhood friends. They went through college together, were very competitive, even when it came to dating. In their senior year they fell in love with the same girl, but L.C., Diana's father, went on to study law at Harvard and that left my father an open field."

"We're talking about your mother, aren't we?" murmured Kendall with a tilt of her head.

"Yes." He dropped his gaze to the candle flickering between them, but saw only images of the past. "It was a good marriage. My father prospered in business. My mother was busy with James and me...."

Kendall made a sound of surprise. "Adam—you had a brother?"

"He died a long time ago in a motorcycle accident. It's still not easy for me to talk about him."

"I understand. Go on, then."

"L.C. came back to town with his bride. Her name was Grace. She smelled of roses." He shook his head and twisted his lips into a wry smile. "It's funny the things that stick with you when you're a kid."

"You liked her."

"I'm not sure I remember her well enough to say whether I did or not; there was just something restful about her. In fact, I remember overhearing my parents talking about how surprised they were that L.C. should marry someone so quiet. In contrast, my mother was like a hummingbird, always on the go, always singing and laughing." He paused to take another sip of his drink.

"To make a long story short, apparently Grace *wasn't* right for L.C., because he seduced my mother into having an affair with him. He even convinced her that he was going to divorce Grace. Then he discovered that Grace had finally become pregnant. Unfortunately my mother had already told my father that she was leaving him, and why.''

"Oh, no."

"Naturally my father was hell-bent on revenge and there was a fight that kept the gossips in town in ammunition for years afterward."

"But that wasn't the worst of it, was it?"

"No. You see, L.C. wouldn't leave Grace when he discovered her condition, and being the type of person she was, she forgave him. She died, though, giving birth to Diana."

"And your mother?" Kendall asked gently.

"She changed—they both did. She became a recluse; sometimes it was days before she'd come out of her room, and it was always to find something else to drink. She died when I was six and James was nine."

"What about your father?"

"He became obsessed with doing anything and everything he could to discredit L.C., and L.C. did the same in return. In that respect I guess the competition never stopped until my father passed away."

Their waiter brought their lunches and Adam ordered himself another Scotch. He glanced down at the prime rib he couldn't remember ordering and wondered if he had the appetite to eat any of it. Then he glanced across the table at Kendall and found her watching him. Her lovely eyes were suspiciously bright.

"It was a long time ago, Kendall. I'm all right."

"Are you?"

He let out a long breath and downed the rest of his drink.

"Adam . . . forgive me if you think I'm overstepping the bounds of friendship here, but you're not blaming Diana for who her father is, are you?"

"I was for a while," he admitted. "But I finally realized what a jerk I was being."

"And you let your true feelings for her surface," Kendall said, after swallowing a bite of her crab salad. "What went wrong?"

"I couldn't *forget* who her father was. And don't tell me it shouldn't matter. It does. You of all people should know that. It may not be very romantic, but when two people get together, there's a whole freight train of baggage that comes along for the ride, ready or not, and hers is a bit hard to cope with."

"How does she feel about yours?" Kendall saw him frown and shook her head sadly. "You're so tied up in your own hurt and anger; did it ever occur to you that she's as much a victim in all this as you were? She lost her mother, too. Of course, there are those who'll say you can't miss what you never had, but take it from me, you can. And as for dumping all the burden of guilt on her father's shoulders, I firmly believe that it takes two consenting individuals to have an affair. Maybe—just maybe—your parents weren't as happy together as you think they were." She saw him stiffen and reached across to lay a soothing hand on his jacket sleeve again. "I'm sorry. I know that might not have been the kindest thing to say, and maybe you should tell me I'm way off in left field and should mind my own business, after all."

"I know you mean well." Adam sighed.

"I only want to see you happy, the way Braden and I are."

"What you have is rare. It doesn't happen for everyone."

She shook her head so that her sleek pageboy brushed against the collar of her pale yellow dress. "It's rare, because we work hard to make it the best it can be." Humor turned her eyes the color of gemstones. "Speaking of which, I have a confidence to share, too. I'm pregnant."

Across the room Diana heard Adam's whoop of delight and looked over to see him rise from his chair and give his luncheon companion an enthusiastic kiss. She pushed away the filet of sole she'd barely touched and gave Martin a look of urgent appeal.

"Yeah," he muttered, raising his napkin to his lips and signaling for their waitress. "I guess you've had about all the atmosphere you can stand for one day."

"I'm sorry, Martin."

"It's okay." He tossed a few bills onto the table and quickly escorted her to the exit. "I'm just disgusted that the fool is too dense to figure out what he's throwing away."

Adam *was* troubled, though at first he tried to tell himself it was only a reaction to Kendall's news about her pregnancy. Delayed reaction to missed opportunities, that's what it was. After all, he was edging in on forty fast. Men were no different from women when it came to those landmark birthdays.

But as the day progressed, he began to acknowledge it went deeper than that. Far deeper.

It wasn't opportunities, but one in particular that had him eating himself up inside. This one had a face and a name, a scent and a taste exclusively her own, and she was preying on his sanity worse than any tropical fever could.

Back at his office he closed files, ignored others and finally watched from his window when the sun went down and people left for the day. He had no reason to leave. He'd found the woman to fill the many empty corners of his life, and he'd walked away from her.

He went to his car and tried to drive away from his thoughts, only to find others.

He had blocked out her pain all these years, blamed her for being a Fontaine, for being talented, for causing him to desire her. Every intellectual rule of logic had been abandoned in order to pacify his own suffering.

He drove for hours, never thinking about the appointment he was breaking. Night fell. He found himself driving down a street he'd avoided for years. His hands began to ache because of the grip he had on the steering wheel, and finally, uttering an oath in resignation, he pulled to the curb and shut off the engine.

How tall the shrubs had grown; he could barely see the whitewashed walls for the shrouding greenery. Only the windows were visible, and he could see that most of the lights inside were turned on. The effect was one of animation, the way a pumpkin became a jack-o'-lantern because someone had put a candle inside to bring the carved face to life. The front door opened. Music spilled into the night—and laughter, young, vibrant laughter. A party was going on. Life was continuing.

He glanced to the house next door. There were no cars in the driveway, lights were few and turned low. The parallel didn't slip by him: the past was fading.

But not quite, he thought, drawing a deep breath. He still carried its bitter seeds inside him. If he continued to nourish them, all he had to look forward to was a house with no lights. Hell, he didn't even have a house; he had a glorified apartment!

I'm not the enemy, Adam.

It takes two to have an affair.

You've been a real sweetheart.

Maybe your parents weren't as happy together as you think.

I love you.

Adam dragged his hand over his face, cursing life in general and himself in particular. Then he turned on the ignition key and drove the Mercedes into the circular driveway of the dimly lit house.

L.C. himself answered the door, dressed in a smoking jacket, his glasses and a book still in hand. But if he looked roused from a pleasant night of reading, he hardly appeared surprised at who had come to call. "Well, Adam," he murmured, neither in welcome nor condemnation.

"I need to talk to you." Tension made the words more a demand than a request.

"About Diana?"

"I don't believe that would be any of your business. I want to talk about you and my parents."

"And I could say that was none of yours."

Adam met the older man's steady gaze without blinking. "But you won't."

For a moment it looked as if L.C. might be tempted to challenge that, but he simply sighed and, murmuring something about young lions, rearranged his bookmark. Stepping aside, he gestured for Adam to enter. As the door closed, more laughter and music drifted over the hedge from next door.

Diana gave a final read through the opening remarks she would make at the Porter trial the following morning. Satisfied she could do no more to improve it, she placed the legal pad on top of the files pertinent to the case and slumped back in her chair. Now, if only she could make it to her bed, she was certain oblivion would be hers.

She slipped off her glasses and rubbed the bridge of her nose. Her eyes felt as if they'd been dipped in margarita salt. The rest of her didn't feel much better. If she survived this case, she was going to take a week or so off, maybe go somewhere quiet, maybe ask L.C. if he wanted to go to see some of the cousins up north.

She pushed herself out of her chair, picked up the plate with the half-eaten sandwich she'd prepared for herself earlier, and turned off the study light. Too bad the neighbor's cat wasn't a dog, she mused, heading for the kitchen. She could help sustain it with her scraps.

She'd just put the plate in the sink when the doorbell rang, causing her heart to skip—a reaction that she quickly scoffed. *Fool, you don't realize when you're better off. He's probably at home finalizing his own plan of attack. That's undoubtedly Martin at the door, checking up on you.* But when she glanced at her watch, she lifted her eyebrows. It was getting late, even for fairy godfathers.

Barefoot, she hurried to the door to peek through the security viewer, and this time her heart did more than skip. Adam, not Martin, stood illuminated in the outside lights, staring into the viewer as if he knew she were there, and was debating what to do.

"Open the door, Diana."

Polite to the end, she thought grimly. She was of a mind to switch off the lights and hope he walked into a low-hanging branch. She didn't want to be seen like this, she thought, glancing down at herself. Her white terry-cloth robe was washed into comfortable but hardly elegant limpness, and her eyes probably looked as if she'd been crying....

"Diana!"

She ground her teeth and unlocked the dead bolt. "Don't you *dare* use that tone of voice with me," she replied, glaring through the six-inch gap she'd opened the door. But her anger was difficult to maintain once she had a chance to get a second look at him. Though still dressed for the office—the navy suit giving credence to the value of fine tailoring—he didn't look in much better shape than she was. His face was drawn, the skin under his eyes bruised from exhaustion. It kindled impulses of tenderness she had to grip the door to resist.

Still, her initial sharpness softened. "Why can't this wait until the morning, Adam?"

The corners of his mouth turned downward in a grim smile. "Because I doubt you'd want the jury, and God knows who else, to listen to us discuss our personal relationship in the middle of the courtroom."

Despite the tingling sensation that skittered down her spine, she kept her voice cool. "We don't have a personal relationship."

"Don't we?" There, that flash of vulnerability—he hated himself for forcing it to surface, but for his own sanity he needed to know it still existed. "Diana, I've just come from talking to L.C. Will you let me come in?"

He was unpredictable in court; why shouldn't that characteristic hold true in his personal life, as well? Knowing she had to hear what this was about, she let him enter. Praying she wasn't making a mistake, she followed him into the living room.

She watched him glance around, note the darkened rooms. In the fluorescent light streaming from the kitchen, his hair seemed frosted with morning dew, leaving silvery streaks her fingers ached to touch. She shoved her hands deep into the pockets of her robe.

"So?"

He turned, let his gaze drift over her. She looked close to dropping from exhaustion, as well as determined to do battle until she did. He wanted to laugh. He wanted to draw the robe off her equally pale shoulders and surround himself with the silk of her body. But he was certain that she would take a swing at him if he tried either.

"Would you like to sit down, get yourself something to drink?"

"What I would *like* is never to have—" She blew out a breath in exasperation. No, she wasn't going to make this messy. Let him say what he'd come to say and then leave. She'd never cried over a man before; this one wouldn't make her do it twice.

"You were going to say you wished you'd never made love with me, is that it?" he asked grimly.

She shot him a bitter glance. "We had *sex*, Adam. It took me a while, but I've gotten it straight now."

Temper flared in him. Before he could stop himself, he grabbed her arm. "Stop it! It was more than that, and we both know it. That's why I reacted the way I did."

Her laugh was brief and cutting. "Of course. How illogical of me not to have realized that."

"For the love of heaven, which one of us are you trying to draw blood from?" he demanded, dragging her the rest of the way into his arms. With desperation mixing with his fury he did the only thing he knew to do to shut her up. He crushed his mouth upon hers, and in the torrent of needs stored up for three days and three decades, he offered her everything.

But Diana was in no condition to see that.

Not again, she vowed. As his mouth devoured hers, she fought to free the arms he trapped at her sides. Not again, she prayed as he bent her backward, cutting her strength, cutting it further by skimming his lips down the vulnerable line of her throat. She squirmed to free herself, but all that did was loosen her robe, giving him more access. When he closed his mouth over her breast, the sweet-sharp pain shot straight through to her spine, causing her body to go rigid before it trembled in pleasure, and she couldn't quite hold back the low moan that rose to her lips.

"You want me. Say it," he demanded, circling with his tongue that which he'd already coaxed into a hard peak.

"Yes. I want you . . . but it doesn't solve anything."

"It's the tie that binds. The rest we'll work out." He scooped her into his arms and carried her to the bedroom, needing the time to regain control. This time he was determined to do it right. For her, he would search beneath the ashes and find tenderness. She would listen then; listen and understand.

The room was dark save for the amber glow emanating from the night-light in the bathroom. It gave the woman in his arms the exotic beauty of an alabaster goddess gilded in gold. As he laid her on the bed and straightened to remove his jacket and tie, he looked his fill at what was now more exposed than covered.

But Diana was more than marble and in no frame of mind to be carried off to bed like a prize. Sitting up, she struggled with the tangle of her robe and rolled herself off the other side of the bed.

"Just hold it right there," she sputtered, dragging the ends of the robe across her breasts. "You think you can say what you said to me the other day, then waltz in here under the pretense of—Adam! Stay where you are or I'll—"

He moved around the bed with the speed of a predator. Before she could escape to the bathroom, he'd caught her, tossed her back onto the bed and pinned her down with his body.

"Will you stop!"

"Will you leave?"

He sighed, relaxing against her. "No, because you don't really want me to," he murmured, releasing one of her wrists to stroke her cheek. "And I don't want to, either."

All too aware of the intoxicating pleasure of having his body pressing against hers, and determined not to let him see it, she turned her head aside. "I won't let you enjoy this."

"You won't be able to help yourself." Lowering his head, he kissed the corner of her mouth, her cheek, traced the delicate shell of her ear with the tip of his tongue. "Love has a tendency to make one generous."

"How would you know?"

"Because I—after spending the last three days in hell—have ascended to that privileged zenith and I must admit I'm feeling incredibly magnanimous."

She shut her eyes tightly. "Adam, I think I prefer your anger to your sarcasm."

"Look at me," he demanded. When she refused, he took hold of her chin and forced her to turn her head. *"Look at me."*

She did, but her expression was mutinous because she had to blink away tears she hadn't wanted him to see. Touched, he was patient, stroking the line of her jaw with the backs of his fingers until he saw the resentment in her eyes give way to disbelief, then hope. But when he saw the doubt return, he frowned and framed her face between his hands.

"No. No doubts. I love you, Diana. If it's the words you need, you'll have them. As many as it takes. Have you ever met an attorney who wasn't long-winded? I love you," he repeated more gently. "I think that's what I went to L.C.'s to face. I told myself it was because I needed to get some answers about the past, but I think it was more to declare myself to him. I thought if I could make him listen, I knew you would."

"And he did?"

"More than I deserved. He even offered me his twenty-year-old brandy to sip on while I worked on removing the chip off my shoulder."

She had to laugh at that. Then, needing to touch, she reached for his hand. He loved her. She could almost hear the echo of it in her racing heartbeat. "Tell me," she murmured. "Tell me what you learned."

He didn't want to dwell on it anymore, not tonight, so he was brief. "You were right. For all these years I've been believing in a lie. Did you know L.C. has some letters from my mother?"

"No, he never told me."

"I didn't want to read them, but he said one in particular was important, so I did." He paused, absently taking her hand to his lips as he sorted the things he wanted to tell her. "My parents weren't happy—I suppose it all comes down to that. It was L.C. my mother loved, L.C. who was the passion in her life, just as she was his. Looking at it from that angle, it's easy to see how both marriages were doomed from the beginning. And it's incredible how fate played such a cruel joke on so many people."

"Maybe some of it was fate, but a lot of it was choices. But, yes, it's sad," Diana added softly. "Especially for you and James. You two suffered the most."

"Do you know all these years I believed she'd rejected me, just as she rejected my father."

"Oh, Adam, no!"

"I hated L.C. for that. He seemed to have everything, and there was nothing left for us."

Diana drew him down to her and held him close. "How awful. The young need so much love. And to think all these years I picked on you for being so remote and cold."

"I was. I wasn't about to give anyone else a chance to reject me—especially after I lost James."

Tears squeezed from the corners of Diana's tightly closed eyes. Adam felt them on his cheek and lifted his head.

"No. No more," he murmured gruffly, kissing them away. "You were right about letting go of the past, too. It's already taken up enough of our lives. Tonight we start fresh. Remember what you said to me the other night? It's haunted me ever since." He brushed his lips across hers once, again. "Love me, Diana. Make love to me as you've never loved anyone before."

His kiss was a promise. It drew his name from her lips in a whisper that trembled like the golden light shim-

mering in the room. Gazes locked, arms entwined, they
drew on the moment sealing it in their memories. Then
she stroked her hands up along his bare back and
smiled, enjoying his immediate response to her. He
ducked his head to nuzzle her shoulder, earning him a
sigh of delight. They were light caresses, touches that
cherished, that were born out of a new realm of understanding.

Together they rid her of her robe, laughed in delight
at the way their hands met and fingers tangled at his
belt. But the laughter soon gave way to deeper emotions and sighs of pleasure as flesh stroked against bare
flesh and heated.

"Do you know how much I've missed you these last
three days?" he breathed, his voice as deep and warm
as the hands he slipped into her hair to hold her still for
a melting kiss. "In my sleep—*when* I slept—I found
myself reaching for you, then waking up in a cold sweat
because you weren't there."

"I'm here now."

Which made his body grow damp for different reasons, he mused, feeling the strain mount as he moved
lower down the warm silk of her throat, across a flut-
tering pulse to the firm curve of her breast.

Yet despite the rising urgency within him, he took his
time to taste and to pleasure. This desire to please, to
give, was so new it made him ache. But what a sweet
ache. Here was what he'd craved, what he'd begun to
believe was not for him. Humbled, he worshiped; enchanted, he adored.

Magic. Diana watched the miracle of it evolve in his
eyes, turning ice to fire and dreams into something tangible. No matter how many nights they might share after this, she promised herself this one would always

stand out among them, because this night he gave her his heart.

"Come into me now," she whispered, drawing him back over her, impatient to have him completely.

"I haven't—"

"*Shh.* You have." She closed her eyes. "You will."

Watching, he entered her and it brought him close, so close. There were no words—until she opened her eyes again.

"Love me."

Neither knew which of them spoke, but then as heat swelled and gathered between them, it no longer mattered. They were together. It was right. The endless hours of emptiness were behind them. *They had to be,* he vowed as he gathered Diana close and took them toward their release.

Nine

Morning came all too soon. They'd set the alarm clock for five in the morning, but when the buzzer sounded, Diana groped blindly to shut it off and snuggled back against Adam.

"Don't do that. My resistance to you isn't any better at dawn that it is at midnight," he mumbled, wrapping an arm around her waist anyway.

"Tell me it isn't time to get up."

He brushed her hair out of the way and pressed a kiss at her nape. "Not for you, sleeping beauty, but I've still got to drive across town, shower and change."

His voice—or maybe it was simply the joy of having him near—brought her fully awake, and she rolled over to face him. "Shower here," she murmured, nuzzling his chest before placing a kiss there. "I'll wash your back for you."

In the soft glow of the night-light they'd left burning, he could see her lips were still slightly swollen from his kisses last night and he gave her an amused, sleepy smile. "Dangerous invitation, my sweet. You already look ravished." But that didn't stop him from drawing her against him and running his hand over her sleek curves. Even that small pleasure thrilled him. He had a feeling it always would. "How on earth am I going to do my thing in the courtroom when you're going to be sitting there reminding me of what I'd rather be doing?"

"Maybe you should consider removing yourself from the case," she suggested pertly.

His chest shook with suppressed laughter, and to punish her he gave her shoulder a playful nip. "I knew it. I've fallen in love with a beautiful, blond conniver."

"Just as long as you realize that description could suit both of us. And speaking of blondes, don't you think it's about time to enlighten me about my competition?"

Adam tucked her head back beneath his chin and frowned. "It's too early for puzzles. Give me a bigger hint. Ow!" he gasped, as she tugged a handful of his chest hair.

"Get out of my bed, varlet," she ordered, rising to her elbow and pointing in regal dismissal.

"Uh-uh. I've decided I like it here." Before she could reply, he wrestled her onto her back and proceeded to punish her with a series of love bites from her neck to her knees until she was writhing and choking in laughter. "What's more important is *you* like me here." When he decided she'd had enough, he hovered over her and simply admired the picture she made, her hair in wild disarray, her chest rising and falling as she took quick gulps of air, her breasts deliciously aroused. "God, I love to look at you," he rasped.

But there was still a question in her eyes. When he saw it, he sighed, realizing this wasn't something she was taking lightly. Wanting to dispel whatever foolish notion she might have come up with, he bent to give her a tender kiss.

"You're talking about the picture on my desk."

"The woman you had lunch with. The woman you kissed in front of your colleagues—something, I might point out, the illustrious district attorney isn't likely to do under normal occasions."

"This wasn't a normal occasion. She just told me my godson was going to get a brother or maybe a sister, come to think of it." He smiled at her stunned expression. "Her name is Kendall Manning, formerly Kendall North, until she married a big cop she was particularly nuts about. She's a friend—one of the few people I call that, as you well know."

"You have a godson," she mused. "I had no idea. I wasn't even sure you liked children."

"Can't stand the little buggers. I tell Matt that every time I see him."

"I'll bet." She gave him a rueful smile. "I was jealous."

He kissed the tip of her nose. "I noticed. If it's any consolation, Prescott gave me a few rough nights." He slid his hand along the gentle slope of her hip, up over her waist and ribs to caress the underside of her breast. "I need to go take that shower," he murmured, nibbling at her lips. "But I don't want to."

"You need the right initiative," she replied, slipping from beneath him. Rising from the bed, she languidly made her way to the bathroom door. There she tossed her hair over her shoulder and gave him a seductive smile.

A slow grin spread across Adam's face. "'Initiative.'" He cleared his throat and swung his feet over the side of the bed. "I sure do like your definitions over Webster's, honey."

Long after Adam had left, a smile lingered on Diana's lips. She'd convinced him to stay for breakfast and now had a mess to clean up before she dressed herself. But it had been worth it. It had been wonderful.

"It's also time to wipe that silly smile off your face and start thinking about what you have to do today," she reminded herself while pouring another cup of coffee. Adam was right—it wasn't going to be easy keeping focused on their jobs when they met later in court— but the seriousness of the case made it imperative. Alice Porter's future rested in her hands; she didn't intend to let her down.

She had the breakfast dishes rinsed off and was stacking them in the dishwasher when she heard someone at the front door. Adam? Maybe he'd forgotten something. But Adam didn't have a key, she thought, hearing the telltale signs of the dead bolt opening.

"Rosie!" She stopped in the middle of the living room and stared as her housekeeper set her tote bag on the floor to close the door behind her. "What are you doing here? You're still supposed to be resting."

"I've had about all the rest I can stand, thank you." While passing a side table she checked it for dust and sniffed in disdain. "Looks like I got back just in time. Here's your paper."

Diana took it and gave her a hug. "You look wonderful."

"I look like a woman who's about to lose her mind. My girls treat me like I'm going senile instead of recovering from a heart attack; Leon treats me like I'm his personal maid. I told them I had enough of that and I was going where I'd be paid to be driven crazy."

"Well, thanks."

Rose chuckled and patted Diana's cheek. "You know I'm only pulling your leg. Come into the kitchen before you spill that coffee, and tell me what's going on while I— Lord, child—" Rose stood in the kitchen doorway and stared agape "—what've you been doing in here?"

Diana ducked her head to take a sip of her coffee. "Just making breakfast."

"Looks like a week's worth of breakfasts, and most of it's stuck on the counters."

"I dropped a few eggs."

Rose looked from the two place mats on the table to Diana. "Got distracted, did you?"

"Something like that."

For a moment the older woman simply stood there scowling, her lips compressed in disapproval. "Well, you *do* look happier than I've seen you in a long time. Do I know him?"

"Adam."

"I don't know any Adam."

"District Attorney Rhodes."

Rose's tote bag made a heavy thump as it hit the floor. "I've got to sit down for this," she muttered, settling on one of the dinette chairs. "We're talking about Justin's boy? The one you said you'd like to mail a polecat to?"

Behind the rim of her cup, Diana's lips curved. "I've had a change of heart."

"Obviously."

"I'm in love with him, Rosie."

Seeing it plainly on her face, the older woman sighed and reached across the table to pat her hand. "Guess I'd better not try to walk in here and surprise you anymore. I don't want to end up surprising myself."

Diana chuckled. "Let me clean up this mess and I'll get out of your way."

"Don't be silly. You sit and read your paper. I'll take care of cleaning up."

"I'm sure if I called your doctor, he'd be happy to tell you that you're not even supposed to be here."

"I don't need any doctor to tell me what I can and can't do," Rose muttered, rising.

Knowing it was useless to argue with her, Diana shook her head and unfolded the newspaper. "So tell me what Leon thinks about— Oh, no!"

Perplexed, Rose turned to see Diana shakily set down her cup. "Baby, what is it?"

Diana shook her head, her gaze transfixed on the headline halfway down the page: "Murder or Manslaughter? D.A.'s Office Claims Former with New Information in Porter Killing." She quickly read through the article written by one of the paper's newer investigative reporters, but even before she was past the first paragraph her mouth compressed into a grim line.

The article was rife with innuendo and supposition, but what had guaranteed it a front-page space was the "informed sources" accreditation. The doctor who treated Alice Porter before she was booked was going to testify for the prosecution, and informed sources advised that it was his expert opinion Mrs. Porter couldn't have used the weapon in question with the injury she had sustained. That, in turn, raised the speculation that perhaps the injury was self-inflicted, occurring after the shooting to support the defendant's claim of having been attacked by the deceased.

Reading over her shoulder, Rose made a disgruntled sound. "How can the paper print something like that? Isn't there a gag order or something to stop them?"

"Gag orders can't be imposed on the press. It constitutes a violation of First Amendment rights. Besides, the jury is sequestered; the paper could easily argue that there's no way they'd be affected by this."

"'The district attorney was unavailable for comment.'"

Diana was staring at that last line, too. "Don't say it," she whispered, swallowing the bitter taste that rose in her mouth.

The phone rang. Muttering under her breath, Rose went to get it. A few moments later she placed her hand over the mouthpiece. "It's him," she mouthed.

Diana closed her eyes. She wasn't surprised; the question was, was the call a pretense or a sign of real concern? Just having to consider the possibility she'd been played for a fool hurt. But it was necessary. Unfortunately there wasn't time to worry about it. There was work to do.

"Tell him—" she rose from her chair, conscious of the fatigue that had returned to her limbs "—tell him the defense isn't available for comment, either."

She expected to see reporters at the courthouse; she found a small mob. Security personnel assisted her in getting past them and into an elevator, but the questions the press fired at her in rapid volley kept echoing in her head all the ride up.

What *was* the true story? She'd like to know herself. She intended to find out.

Phil Gresham was waiting for her the moment she stepped from the elevator. "He wants to see you," he said without preamble. "If you'll go up to his office, I'll bring him right to you."

"Where is he now?"

"In the courtroom—just in case you refused."

"Too bad he doesn't follow his instincts more often."

Court wasn't due to convene for another twenty-five minutes and the room was almost empty, but Diana knew her gaze would have zeroed in on Adam regardless. He was dressed somberly in dark gray—appropriate, she thought. As if he could feel her eyes, he turned and, murmuring something to his assistant beside him, joined her. She placed her briefcase on the table reserved for the defense counsel and did her best to avoid his penetrating look. She needed a minute more; her heart was pounding too hard; the hurt she was feeling was too close to the surface.

"I'd have thought you too fair to wear white well, but you look lovely," he murmured, his gaze a caress.

"It's my Joan of Arc outfit," she muttered, explaining the short-jacketed suit. "Rather suitable under the circumstances, don't you think?"

The sting in her words cut Adam like a whip. He stiffened, but managed to keep his voice low. "You should have gone up to my office. I could have explained things to you."

"With a rosebud, or were you going to spring for the whole dozen this time?" Wincing, Diana made a quick gesture rejecting the rude remark. "I told myself the last thing I was going to do was get personal."

"I want it personal," Adam replied with quiet intensity. "I want you to keep thinking about us so you'll realize there's no way I would pull something like this on you." Someone took a seat in the first row of visitors' benches and Adam led Diana to a more private corner of the room, but his expression turned grim as she carefully disengaged herself from his hold. "Diana, this was as much of a surprise to me as it was to you."

"Please don't insult my intelligence."

"All right, I told Gresham to go talk to the doctor. It was a fluke; he was an intern, close to Phil's age, they hit it off."

"A regular Tom Sawyer and Huckleberry Finn," Diana drawled. "Maybe *you* should be wearing the white suit."

Adam let that pass. Barely. "Phil took him to a bar near the hospital. It was supposed to be just a routine follow-up type of thing. We didn't think he'd be any real source of information. We were more interested in what the medical examiner had to say about Porter's autopsy, but routine's routine."

"You'll understand if I don't feel compelled to applaud your staff's sudden streak of assiduousness—or to buy this, for that matter."

As she began to step away, Adam grabbed her arm. "Phil didn't know someone had sat down in the booth behind him. He also didn't know the intern was a paperback-mystery junkie and that he'd already been having second thoughts about the night the cops brought Alice Porter in to be treated. And he *did* try to reach me—only by then I was with you. Had I learned about this first, I would have come to you and we could have quietly worked this out—let Alice change her plea, whatever."

"Change her plea? You must be joking."

"Diana—for the love of heaven—you read the article. An *expert* says there's no way she could have used that gun with her hand broken like that. *The break must have occurred after Porter was shot.*"

"Excuse me—" the bailiff who interrupted shuffled and gave them each an embarrassed glance "—Judge Canfield wants to see you in her office."

"Great," Adam muttered. "What else?"

"Don't forget the part about your intern being a mystery junkie," Diana said, her voice laced with sarcasm. "She could probably use a good laugh, too."

Judge Canfield sat behind her desk making no pretense of hiding her displeasure or the newspaper before her. Her mouth was pinched; behind her tortoiseshell glasses, her hazel eyes were dark with censure. Diana was fleetingly reminded of the mother superior in *The Sound of Music*, but she doubted Lenore was going to do any singing about climbing mountains and following rainbows.

As soon as the bailiff shut the door, she slipped off her glasses and motioned for both attorneys to sit down. "We've just spent a week of taxpayers' money—not to mention their time—trying to secure an unbiased jury to try this case. Now I see the press is more than happy to do our job for us." She dropped her voice a half octave and tapped the paper with her frames. "Would one of you mind enlightening me about what is going on here?"

Adam did with impressive brevity and without following Diana's suggestion. "We will want to subpoena Dr. Sebring," he added. "Unless counsel and her client would like to rethink their position and move on to sentencing."

"What counsel would like," Diana ground out, "is not to have her client's testimony, indeed her *character*, impugned by one overworked, underexperienced intern. I thought it was the purpose of a trial to hear *all* testimony, not simply to choose a purported expert's opinion and swallow it hook, line and sinker."

Adam turned sideways in his seat. Didn't she realize what she was doing? She was cutting him in two. She was telling him she was willing to fight him on this one; and if that happened, what would be left of their relationship to piece back together? "I won't let you do this to us," he said quietly. But not so quietly that Lenore Canfield couldn't hear, and when Diana shot her a worried glance, he turned to her himself. "Judge, I know this is highly irregular, but could we have a few minutes alone?"

The older woman glanced from him to Diana, noticed the twin spots of color spreading on her cheeks and raised her penciled eyebrows. Sighing, she collected her glasses and the paper, then rose. "And my kids think I've got a mundane job," she muttered. "You've got ten minutes."

"How could you?" Diana demanded, even as the adjoining door leading to another room closed.

Adam glared back at her. "It was easy. All I had to do was think back to earlier this morning and remember the way you went crazy with my hands and mouth all over you."

"That's not fair."

"Neither is what you're doing. What you *will be* doing if you go through with this."

"What am I doing?" Diana cried, rising to relieve some of the tension bubbling inside her. "I'm trying to secure my client a fair trial!"

THAT FONTAINE WOMAN! 171

"You're not seeing the handwriting on the wall, and you're willing to risk *us* in the process." Adam joined her by the bookshelves containing the judge's extensive collection of legal opinions and lightly took her by the shoulders. "Please, just hear me out."

How could she not when his voice had the same husky urgency as when he was close and eager to satisfy her. She swallowed, her throat dry. "Like Lenore said, you've got ten minutes."

He released her, because it was safer that way, and he even took a few steps away. "I don't believe Alice Porter's life was in mortal danger the night she shot her husband. Yes," he added quickly as Diana turned around to protest, "Carl probably deserved to be the one put behind bars. Yes, I can read between the lines and see he was drunk more than he was sober, and yes, I know he was violent. But as the medical examiner clearly states in his report, it's conceivable—no, probable—that Porter was too drunk that night to have posed a threat to anything or anyone except the piece of furniture he might eventually have landed on *if* he had lived long enough to pass out."

"Statistics do not substantiate guilt," Diana reminded him. "Readings of the alcohol level in the blood don't take into consideration a person's height, weight, body mass.... Porter was six foot four and weighed two hundred and thirty pounds!"

"And he was known to become more violent the more he drank, I know." Adam ran his hand over the hair at his nape. "But this night was different. This night he let a buddy drive him home, because even *he* knew he was close to his limit."

"Next you're going to suggest Alice gave herself those cuts and bruises on her face," Diana said bitterly.

"No. I believe he did that. She could have lit into him the minute he walked through the front door, done something to set him off. He backhanded her and his ring opened her lip; the force of the blow sent her into the corner by the kitchen door. It could have been the last straw for her. She went into the kitchen where she'd already placed the gun beside the box of bullets the police found and . . ." He gestured vaguely.

"Then afterward she was supposed to break her own hand?" Diana shook her head. "Do you realize what kind of person you're describing?"

"A desperate one," Adam admitted, his expression compassionate. "One who had been in hospital five times in the last two years. One who realistically feared for the safety of her infant daughter and who went so far as to assure her protection by having her stay with her sister that night. One who made the place look like there'd been a war, though her husband's body was found three or four steps into the house. Diana, the blow to her hand was caused by a blunt object and it made a clean break. I have the X-rays if you want to see them. There was nothing found in the immediate vicinity that could have done that kind of damage, and there was no way Alice was going to hold that gun steady in that hand, let alone pull the trigger. It's usually the inability of a perpetrator to think things through clearly that allows us to catch them; but I have to admit I'm not getting any pleasure out of resolving this one."

Diana felt as if she'd just stepped into an uncovered manhole, except that on the ride down, instead of blackness there was a visual replay of everything Adam just told her. It was no less disturbing the second time around, and what was shattering was that she began to see what before she'd been—what?—ignoring? God, she was a lawyer. It was her job to see details, facts, the hidden.

"There's just one more thing," Adam said, coming closer. He didn't like the way she seemed to be shutting down like a computer that had been asked to do too much. He closed his hand around the nape of her neck, slanted his mouth over hers and kissed her. It wasn't a gentle kiss, either. Desperate men did desperate things. Adam could feel he was about to go under the microscope along with Alice Porter, and that his past sins were still too fresh not to show like moon craters in a telescope. He needed an edge. She loved him. He needed her to hold on to that.

The kiss went on and on; demanding, entreating. When he heard the discreet knock at the door, he almost swore because he could feel her resisting him. But as he slowly lifted his head, he also saw the helpless arousal in her dilated eyes.

"While you're thinking, think about that," he muttered, his breath coming in shallow gulps. He walked out before she had time to recover and reply.

Another knock sounded and Lenore Canfield poked her head into the room. "Diana? You okay?"

"No." Diana ran a hand across her forehead, not at all surprised to find it damp. "Lenore, read me the riot act if you have to, but I have to speak with my client before we walk into that courtroom again."

The room was an ugly beige, unimproved by the heavily barred windows or the fluorescent overhead lights. Diana sat down at the huge table in the center of the room, only because her legs felt like overcooked macaroni. It was the heat, she tried to tell herself; they always made these rooms too hot.

A female guard brought Alice soon afterward, taking her place by the door, a visible but dispassionate observer. Diana wondered about the tales *she* could tell, and shifted her gaze to her client.

Today Alice was in civilian clothes, in an outfit picked out by her sister at a local discount store. It was dubious whether the blue print dress with its pleated skirt and little-girl collar might have done something for the mannequin at the store—it certainly didn't do anything for Alice. She was a tall woman, finely boned, gaunt. Her brown hair was limp and cut blunt at her ears. She tucked it behind them at regular intervals, though it never seemed to want to stay put. Her face was narrow, her best features being her deep-set brown eyes and her skin. Alice had a lovely, camellia-white complexion. In the right clothes and with the right makeup, she would have been considered a handsome woman. But Carl Porter never liked to see his wife in "paint," and as a result, Alice's face was just *there*.

"Hello, Alice. Come sit down."

"Aren't we going into the courtroom?"

"Yes, but I need to talk to you first. Please—come sit down."

Alice took the seat at Diana's left, nervously fiddling with the bandages on her right hand. "Have you seen my sister yet?"

"She's already outside. Is the hand giving you trouble?"

"No. It throbs a little, but that's all right." Alice glanced from Diana to the newspaper on the table and back again. "Is there something in there about me?"

"Yes, and I'm afraid it's going to give us a lot of trouble. That's why I wanted to meet with you first." Diana caught the guard's eye, indicated the paper and shifted it toward her client. "Read this. It should be self-explanatory."

Alice was a slow reader, which gave Diana plenty of time to watch her. The cut on her lip had healed; the one by her right eye, because of the stitches, was healing a bit more slowly. However, what Diana was sensitive to wasn't Alice's injuries but her nerves; she was looking for a sign to tell her how to proceed.

"Dr. Sebring," Alice murmured, smiling briefly as she recognized the name. "He was nice to me." But a moment later the smile turned into a frown. She marked her place with her index finger and looked up at Diana. "Why would he want to say something like this?"

"The doctor was merely speaking as a trained observer, Alice. He sees many different kinds of injuries come through that emergency room, and in a way he studies them the way he did the body and diseases in medical school, because he needs to know how much the body can take before it can't function correctly." Diana paused, for once in her life unable to find the right words. "Your injuries disturbed him," she said at last.

"He's saying what happened didn't happen," Alice corrected. She drew her bottom lip between her teeth, thinking. "He's going to testify against me, isn't he?"

"It's my understanding the district attorney is going to subpoena him to testify as an expert witness, yes."

"Expert?" Thrusting the newspaper away, Alice jumped to her feet. "He wasn't there. He doesn't know!"

"Easy, Porter," the guard warned.

Alice shot her a resentful look and began pacing around the room. "Do you know there've been doctors who've treated me and told me I'm lucky to be alive?

Where are *those* experts, Ms. Fontaine? You can't let them do this to me. I've got a baby out there who needs me."

Resting her elbows on the table, Diana massaged her temples with the pads of her fingers, though she knew it would take a lot more to relieve the tension headache beginning to throb there. She had seen little Bonnie, had gone to visit Alice's sister to make sure the child was being properly cared for and to offer whatever assurances she could. It was part of what she believed was services due a client. Because she cared. Because she believed. But as L.C. had often warned her, it was making things difficult now.

"Alice, let me tell you what the D.A. is going to hit you with when we go out there." Without mincing words, she laid it all out for her, and as she did, Alice became more and more distraught.

"It's not *fair*," Alice cried, wrapping her arms around herself. "They don't see anything but what they want to see. I went through hell with that man. He was no good." Tears began to flood her eyes and spilled unheeded down her face. Moaning softly, she went back to her pacing. "He didn't care if I had food for the baby... money to pay the doctor. I just couldn't take anymore. I couldn't."

Diana's heart felt like a wrecking ball beating against her breastbone, but she remained seated and kept her voice calm. "What happened, Alice?"

"I told you!" the younger woman screamed.

"Porter!"

The guard took a step toward Alice. Diana quickly signaled to her that it was all right.

"I know what you told me," she said wearily. "But now I want you to tell me again, and then again. And remember, it's going to be the story you'll tell the judge and the jury *after* they hear that Carl was so drunk that night, he was ready to pass out on the living-room couch—if he could have made it that far."

"Oh, God—he was sober enough to do this," Alice sobbed, pointing to her eye. "Would it have been better if he'd killed *me*? *Would it?*"

"You know better than to ask that."

"All right! You want the truth? I'll give it to you. I did it. Premeditated or whatever fancy words you people use for unpleasant things," she sobbed, leaning across the table. "And you want to know something else? I'd do it again."

"Now tell me how you really hurt your hand."

As quickly as it surfaced, Alice's anger dissolved. She withdrew to a huddled figure standing in the corner.

"It was the car door."

"Afterward?"

Unable to speak because of a new rush of tears, she nodded. "It was an accident," she managed in a strangled voice. She wiped her cheeks with the back of her good hand. "I began t-to think I should have Bonnie with me s-so I was going to get her, and then the phone rang. I slammed the door—I was confused. It hurt."

Diana closed her eyes for a moment.

"Ms. Fontaine, I know you think what I did was wrong, but you have to understand I had no choice. I just knew I had to get it over with that night."

"You had a choice, Alice."

"That's not true!"

When Diana opened her eyes again, they were bleak but direct. "There are homes for women in your situation. I've placed some people there myself. There are also support groups. There *were* other choices."

Alice turned away and stepped to the window to stare at the nearly cloudless sky. "I have to go out there, don't I? I have to tell them?"

"Yes."

"Will—will you be with me?"

"Yes, Alice. I'll be right beside you."

Ten

It felt like déjà vu. Her car was in the driveway but she wasn't answering the door. At least this time he knew the routine, he thought, circling the front to go around to the back. What he should have done is come here first to begin with, instead of going to her office. He should have known she wouldn't be in any mood for work. But he couldn't imagine her walking on the beach, either.

He found her sitting on the back deck, her legs up on the railing—an alluring picture, since she didn't seem to be wearing much more than a short lavender robe. But he frowned when he saw the bottle of vodka on the table beside her.

"What's that going to prove?" he asked, climbing the stairs to join her.

She glanced over her shoulder. She'd known he would come, but just wasn't sure she was ready to see him.

Even so, the sight of him made her pulse quicken. Hail the conquering hero, she mused, noting the arrogant way he carried his jacket flipped over his right shoulder.

"Well?"

"What?"

"I asked you what this was supposed to prove," he said again, tossing his jacket into another chair and picking up the bottle of vodka.

"Not a damned thing, but it may shut down my head for a few hours."

Adam set down the bottle. "Feeling sorry for yourself?"

"If you've come to gloat," she replied, returning pained eyes to the calm surf, "or to tell me 'I told you so,' I think I should warn you that now isn't the best time."

Without warning, Adam snatched the glass she was holding out of her hand and tossed the contents over the railing. "Damn it, knock it off! You hate this stuff."

"I hate wasting money, too, and that was, after all, imported, comrade." She extended her hand. "May I have my glass back, please? Come on, Adam. I have it on good authority that one good drink does not a lush make, and if you add plenty of ice, it isn't half-bad."

He glanced at the dent she'd made in the bottle already. "Uh-uh," he decided. "You've had enough. Any more and you won't hear a word I say to you."

"Hint, hint."

He set the glass on the railing out of reach and crossed his arms over his chest. "Okay. Get it out of your system. You want to shout, shout; you want to cry, I've got a strong shoulder; you want to take a swing at me, just remember—the payback's hell."

"Don't make me laugh," she muttered, quickly looking away. "Why can't you just go away and leave me alone to work this out for myself?"

"Because I happen to know the Diana Fontaine I've come to care about would probably volunteer to shoulder a lot of blame that's not hers." When that didn't get the reaction he'd hoped for, he dropped his head back in frustration and sighed. "Okay, so you were wrong. So you discovered you were fallible—"

"Oh, I'm fallible all right." Her laugh was bitter. "First I blow it with Leon and now this. If she hadn't confessed..." Diana gave him a tortured look. "Adam, I'd have gone to the wire for her. I would have *won* her an acquittal."

"Are you sure? Look who you were up against." She gave him a dour look, but he ignored it because the phone began to ring. "Don't you want to get that?" he asked, when she made no move to rise.

"No."

"It might be your office."

"Undoubtedly it's a reporter. Why don't you go pull the plug?"

He did go in, but he chose instead to answer the phone. Gut instincts. It was L.C.

"Yeah, I'm staying," he said after a moment, watching her through the opened French doors. "Whether she likes it or not.... What...? Sounds good to me."

Diana would never admit that she'd listened, but when he returned a moment later, she was bristling. "I don't need baby-sitting."

"That was L.C."

Immediately her tone changed to one of concern. "Is he all right?"

"Funny, that's exactly what he asked about you."

Caught, Diana lifted her chin and glanced back out to sea. "You needn't worry. I've already lost my desire to drown my troubles. Why don't you go away and celebrate or something?"

"Some cases you don't celebrate; you just try to accept them and get on with your life," he replied quietly.

He understood. Why had she worried he wouldn't? "Adam, what if I've been kidding myself? What if all those high-minded principles I've touted have been nothing more than ego?"

He wanted to hold her. He wanted to go down on his knees, put his arms around her and hold her. Instead, he managed a crooked smile. "Would I fall in love with a jerk?"

Her expression went from stunned to indignant. Then humor crept in. "Oh, no. Not you."

They both burst into laughter, but when he saw tears shimmering in her eyes, Adam extended his hand. "Come here." In the next instant she was in his arms and he held her close, tightly. "I'm sorry," he whispered against her hair. "One of us had to lose, but I'm sorry you got hurt in the process. And whether you're ready to believe it or not, you're going to survive *and* become a better lawyer for it."

"Oh, God, I need you," she whispered, holding him close.

Had anything ever sounded so sweet? He swallowed with difficulty. "Good. Because I need you, too. At least we're smart enough to figure that out."

A typical Rhodes response. She wanted to laugh again, but different emotions came into play. Blame it on the alcohol.

"Adam?"

"Yeah?"

No, it was more than that, she thought, hearing the strain rising in his voice. She stroked her cheek against his. "Just this," she whispered, searching for and finding his mouth. His lips were warm, welcoming, and she went on tiptoe to deepen the kiss.

It was everything he wanted—and more. He slid his hands down over the slender hips shifting provocatively against his. "Be careful," he muttered. "I'm not sure which one of us is more vulnerable." But she didn't stop and a few moments later he had to drag his mouth free to catch his breath. "Inside?"

"The last time you said that to me it wasn't a question."

"Caveman tactics. The last time I was half-afraid you'd have second thoughts and send me away. No one's ever been inside me as deep as you are, love."

Joy does have a place beside grief, she realized, taking his hand. Smiling, she led him inside.

"Where's Rose?" Adam asked, as they passed the sparkling kitchen and he remembered the delicious but messy breakfast they'd shared earlier.

"I sent her home. We've agreed on her working only half a day for a while, until she's gotten her strength back."

"Nice lady."

"Mmm."

She was reaching to turn down the bed and he drew her back into his arms. "I meant you."

She ran her hands over his chest, thrilling to the way his chest expanded as he dragged in a deep breath, the way his heart began to pound. "I don't want to feel 'nice' right now," she murmured, untying his tie. She left it draped around his neck to unbutton his shirt, placing warm kisses over every inch of tanned flesh she exposed. "I want to feel hot and achy and I want to make you feel that way, too."

Adam ran his hands up her thighs, beneath the hem of her robe, slipping them under the elastic and silk of her panties. "Proceed to step *B*," he suggested gruffly.

"I want to drive us both over the edge," she whispered, her breath scorching his flat nipples before tormenting him further with her tongue. "Until it hurts, Adam. Until it hurts to touch as much as it hurts not to."

"Everything."

"You . . . inside me. That's everything."

He never loved her more than at that moment. Hurt, vulnerable, needing a release, needing hope—she looked to him. A future could be built on this, a damn fine one.

"Marry me," he whispered, ducking his head to seek her lips.

Her hands stilled on the waistband of his slacks. "Oh, Adam. I didn't mean—"

"What?"

"You're here. That's all I care about. You don't have to say things you might regret later."

"Remind me to toss out the rest of that vodka later on," he muttered, forcing her backward onto the bed and securing her there with his own body.

"But I don't—"

"No, you don't. So listen up. Better yet, I'll show you."

He supposed she was always going to drive him crazy, he thought, locking his mouth to hers. If not one way, then another. Just when he believed her to be a witch, she turned angel. Just when he wondered if nothing could break her, she scared the hell out of him by almost coming apart. He thought she understood what he meant when he said he needed her, but the darling idiot had obviously experienced a short circuit in her deductive reasoning mode.

And so was he, he realized moments later as the kisser became the kissed. He groaned and slid his hands into her hair to get more. He would die wanting the taste of her on his lips, and how could so much heat come from such a delicate touch?

As it always did, things quickly grew intense between them. Soon it was no longer enough to hold; they had to explore, and Adam made short work of untying Diana's robe, then reaching beneath her to lift her toward his mouth while drawing it from her shoulders.

From breast to thigh he loved her until, naked and trembling beneath him, he ran his hand over her, whispering to her to finish undressing him. And then it started all over again, but this time it was Adam who was the beneficiary of delights that only they could bring to each other.

He thought he might die from it. The caress of her hair on his thighs alone was magnificent agony. She proved there could be much more.

Close, he rolled her beneath him. "I love you," he whispered, his voice strained as he settled between her legs.

"I love you."

Eagerly she reached for him, but he held back stroking her with his hand where she needed much more. "Marry me," he demanded.

"Adam—"

"Say it."

"Yes!"

The word was cut off by a gasp as he surged forward, taking possession so powerfully that control proved impossible. There was only time for Adam to take her mouth in a wild kiss as together they soared toward delirious relief.

Her smile came effortlessly. Even before their hearts began to slow, she felt it. Just as she felt the warm glow of happiness swell inside her, and the amusement. *He had asked*. Well, barely; but she decided she liked the demand, too.

"I see you're adjusting to the idea," Adam mused, smiling as he raised himself onto his elbow.

"Yes." She brushed his hair back from his forehead, adding mischievously, "So where's my ring?"

He burst into laughter. "God, I'm crazy about you. Or maybe I'm just crazy." He sighed, rolling onto his back and taking her with him. "Cut a man no quarter unless he's got the goods. I think our daughters' futures will be safe in your hands."

"Very funny." She tried to look indignant but decided she was too happy to bother. "Daughters, huh? Maybe they'll be sons."

Content, Adam raised her hand to his lips. "Maybe they'll be both. And we'll go this afternoon to pick out a ring," he added. "Do you think I'd do something like that without you?"

"After—" Diana bit her lip. "Oh, Adam, do you think we could go tell my father? He'd be so delighted."

"Sure. But it's not going to be the surprise you think it is."

"What do you mean?" She saw the self-congratulatory smirk on his face and narrowed her eyes. "How? *When?*"

"Just a little while ago on the phone. Didn't you hear me tell him 'Sounds good to me'?" Adam paused for effect. "He wanted to know if he should hurry and send his tuxedo to the cleaners."

"Why that—" Diana gave in to the laughter bubbling up inside her. "Well. It looks like I'm trading in one bossy man for another, doesn't it?"

Adam gently pushed her back against the pillows and gave her a tender kiss. "Yeah, but something tells me you'll be able to handle it."

* * * * *

Keepsake

Harlequin Books

You're never too young to enjoy romance. Harlequin for you . . . and Keepsake, young-adult romances destined to win hearts, for your daughter.

Pick one up today and start your daughter on her journey into the wonderful world of romance.

Two new titles to choose from each month.

FOUR UNIQUE SERIES
FOR EVERY WOMAN YOU ARE . . .

Silhouette Romance

Love, at its most tender, provocative, emotional . . . in stories that will make you laugh and cry while bringing you the magic of falling in love.

Silhouette Special Edition

Sophisticated, substantial and packed with emotion, these powerful novels of life and love will capture your imagination and steal your heart.

Silhouette Desire

Open the door to romance and passion. Humorous, emotional, compelling—yet always a believable and sensuous story—Silhouette Desire never fails to deliver on the promise of love.

Silhouette Intimate Moments

Enter a world of excitement, of romance heightened by suspense, adventure and the passions every woman dreams of. Let us sweep you away.

SILG-1R

ATTRACTIVE, SPACE SAVING BOOK RACK

Display your most prized novels on this handsome and sturdy book rack. The hand-rubbed walnut finish will blend into your library decor with quiet elegance, providing a practical organizer for your favorite hard-or soft-covered books.

Only $9.95

Approximately 16" x 8" when assembled

Assembles in seconds!

To order, rush your name, address and zip code, along with a check or money order for $10.70* ($9.95 plus 75¢ postage and handling) payable to *Silhouette Books*.

Silhouette Books
Book Rack Offer
901 Fuhrmann Blvd.
P.O. Box 1396
Buffalo, NY 14269-1396

Offer not available in Canada.

BKR-2A

*New York and Iowa residents add appropriate sales tax.

Silhouette Desire

1989
IS THE YEAR
OF THE MAN!

What makes a romance? A special man, of course, and Silhouette Desire celebrates that fact with *twelve* of them! From Mr. January to Mr. December, every month spotlights the Silhouette Desire hero—our **MAN OF THE MONTH.**

Sexy, macho, charming, irritating…irresistible! Nothing can stop these men from sweeping you away. Created by some of your favorite authors, each man is custom-made for pleasure—*reading* pleasure—so don't miss a single one.

Diana Palmer kicks off the new year, and you can look forward to magnificent men from **Joan Hohl, Jennifer Greene** and many, many more. So get out there and find your man!

Silhouette Desire's

MAN OF THE MONTH…